# KEELBOATS NORTH

## William Heuman

## Center Point Publishing
### Thorndike, Maine

This Center Point Large Print edition
is published in the year 2004 by arrangement with
Golden West Literary Agency.

Copyright © 1953 by Fawcett Publications, Inc.
Copyright © renewed 1981 by the Estate of William Heuman.

The text of this Large Print edition is unabridged. In other
aspects, this book may vary from the original edition. Printed in
Thailand. Set in 16-point Times New Roman type.

ISBN 1-58547-489-4

Library of Congress Cataloging-in-Publication Data

Heuman, William.
    Keelboats north / William Heuman.--Center Point large print ed.
        p. cm.
    ISBN 1-58547-489-4 (lib. bdg. : alk. paper)
    1. Large type books.  I. Title.

PS3558.E7997K44 2004
813'.54--dc22

2004006250

## Chapter One

It was raining lightly, and there was a mist on the river as Scot MacGregor stepped across the plank from the keelboat Osage and started up along the levee, slipping and stumbling a little in the mud and the darkness here. Behind him he left two of his soberest, most dependable keelboatmen guarding the plank, rifles in hand, preventing the other French Creoles from going ashore and heading for the cribs and taverns of this town of St. Louis, the wickedest city in the West in the year 1832.

Turning east up one of the dark, narrow, muddy streets, Scot heard someone coming behind him, sloshing through the mud, and he immediately stepped back against the wall of a building, his right hand moving inside his coat to touch the bone handle of the pistol stuck in his waistband. The town was full of footpads who would be unusually busy on a concealing, overcast night like this.

Standing there against the building, peering into the shadows, he caught the smell of the town and the dank, damp smell of the river, and he wrinkled his nose in distaste, wishing already that they were eight hundred miles up the Missouri in sight of the big mountains with snow on the peaks, and the air clean and crisp, sweet with the smell of sage and buffalo grass. He had no use for towns and ramshackle buildings, and the foul odor of unwashed men and the holes in which they lived.

The man behind him in the lane had stopped also, and then a voice reached out toward Scot, a drawling, laconic voice with a faint Scotch burr to it:

"That you, Scot?"

"Come ahead, Jonas," Scot told him, and Jonas Keene, who had signed on as hunter on this journey up the Missouri to the fur country, came into the alley.

"Saw you leavin' the boat," Jonas said. "Figured you'd be out lookin' fer that damned Baptiste again tonight."

The hunter was a lean, angular shape in the dim light, his buckskins a gray color in the darkness here. He wore a wolfskin cap, and even here in the town he carried his long-barreled Kentucky rifle, a flintlock weapon that had been converted to percussion.

"Can't leave without Baptiste," Scot said. "Rather go without half a dozen of the others."

Jonas Keene fell in step with him, and together they moved on up to the main street, the dim lights of taverns and house windows glowing through the lightly falling rain.

"Four days an' nights lookin' fer that big Frenchman," Jonas growled, "an' all the while Cass Brandon is makin' tracks upriver. He'll be on the Yellowstone afore we leave St. Louis, Scot."

"We'll catch him," Scot said. "Baptiste Pivot is the best boss-man on the Missouri, and we have a good crew."

They walked along the main street, Scot stopping now and then to look in through a tavern door. He paused once to roll over a drunk who had fallen and lay snoring against the wall of a building, and then went on again, Scot thinking now of Cass Brandon, bourgeois for the

6

Great Western Fur Company, whose keelboat, Yellow-stone Gal, had cast off hawsers four days ago. Brandon would be driving his French Creoles like a madman, anxious to reach the tribes on the upper river first, and reap the big profits. He knew Brandon; he'd wintered once with the big blond man up on the Green River when both of them had been free trappers. He'd seen what Brandon had done to the hapless Flathead Indian who had come looking for the wife Brandon had stolen from him. An Indian without hands was not an Indian—neither good nor bad. Scot MacGregor hoped the Flathead was dead now.

"Brandon beats us up to the Sioux country," Jonas Keene was saying, "an' you'll know what to expect, Scot. He'll have enough liquor aboard to git every Sioux buck in the territory drunken mad, an' waitin' fer the next boat to come along."

"We'll catch him," Scot asserted, "before he's above the Platte."

"If you ketch Baptiste tonight," Jonas growled. "We ain't caught him yet."

They walked on up the almost deserted street, Scot with his heavy Mackinaw coat buttoned around his neck, making him look heavier in the shoulders than he was. He was a big man, inches taller than Jonas Keene, who was nearly six feet tall himself, and he walked with the light, easy tread of a man who was accustomed to walking the deer trails, and not the rutted streets of a big town.

He'd handled many a pole on a keelboat before he became bourgeois for the Empire Fur Company, and he'd developed a body of steel and sinew. When a drunk staggered out of one of the nearby taverns and collided with him, the drunk bounced back and fell into the mud, cursing.

"Four days an' nights missin'," Jonas Keene said glumly. "That Frenchie's likely got enough liquor in him now to float a keelboat. He won't be any good fer a week anyway, Scot."

"If we find him tonight," Scot said, "he'll be the best man on the boat in the morning. I know Baptiste."

"Whole damn boat," Jonas said. "Whole damn Empire Fur Company waitin' on one lousy French Creole who's been celebratin' like he's already come back from a trip upriver, instead o' just startin' on one."

It was more than the boat and the fur company, Scot MacGregor was thinking. It was the whole United States government waiting on one ignorant keelboatman while he finished his drinking bout. The Empire Fur Company's expedition up the Missouri had the sanction of the State Department of the government, which was anxious to preserve the huge Oregon Territory for the United States.

The Osage was headed up the Missouri, deep in the Oregon country now in dispute between the United States and England. They were to go beyond the last Army post on the river and set up a trading post in the Blackfoot country, where no American trading posts existed, and this was to be the first of a string of posts to be set up by the big Empire Fur Company—links in a chain that would stretch to the Pacific, and eventually consolidate the vast territory for the United States.

Fresh back from a trapping expedition to the Three Forks, Scot had listened to Empire Fur officials discuss the matter with government agents in St. Louis. For years the United States and England had disputed claim to the Oregon Territory, and twice they had signed agreements calling for joint occupation. Now with Americans sifting up into the Northwest, the matter eventually would have to be resolved, and that nation with the most settlers and the most trading posts to encourage the settlers would win out.

As one of the government men had put it, "The more Americans we have in the territory, gentlemen, the less chance there is of anyone putting us out. These posts you intend to set up are of tremendous importance.

Scot MacGregor, who had made three keelboat trips upriver for Empire Fur, had been chosen to head the first expedition up into the virgin territory and set up the first post. This time he was not to come back, and walking along the muddied main street in the town of St. Louis this rainy night he was glad. He'd spent the long winter here and in New Orleans, and he'd had enough of cities and houses, and people who lived like cattle. The shining mountains beckoned to him, and the deep, cool woods, and the sparkling streams teaming with beaver.

Jonas Keene said, "Red Lion up ahead, Scot. Seen Baptiste in there many a time. That hoss likes the liquor, an' a little French gal by the name o' Lorraine."

"He wasn't there yesterday," Scot said. "I looked in."

The Red Lion was a two-story frame building occupying the next corner, one of the few two-story buildings in the town, and the largest tavern. Nightly, it was jammed with singing *voyageurs* who bragged of their journeys up into the country of the dread Blackfeet.

A crude painting of a red lion hung over the doorway, raindrops dripping from it, the sign swaying and creaking when a breeze from the river moved it.

When they pushed in through the door, the stench of whisky and tobacco and sweating men struck them like a blow in the face. There was a jumble of voices in French and Spanish, high and shrill, and then the deeper language of the high mountains, the English of the free trappers.

A fat, greasy-faced man with wide, sweeping mustaches stood behind the bar, smiling, filling glasses. Pushing his way between two of the Creoles at the bar, Scot said, "Baptiste Privot been in, Leon?"

"*Non,*" Leon smiled. "*Comment allez-vous,* Monsieur MacGregor?" He pushed a bottle and a glass toward Scot and looked at him approvingly.

Jonas Keene had taken up with a wizened little mountain man in a moth-eaten Mackinaw and fur cap, who had evidently just come in to town. Scot watched them for a moment and then poured himself a drink. He stood at the bar, the reddish hair under his black, flat-crowned hat catching the gleam of yellow lamplight in the room. His face was wide with solid jaws and a long, straight mouth. There was a dent in the bridge of his nose, which would have been straight and well shaped otherwise.

His pale blue eyes moved constantly as he stood at the bar, the liquor glass in his hand, half turning to watch the crowd. They were the eyes of a man who had spent five years of his life in the big mountains, braving the snows

10

and the infinitely more dangerous Blackfeet. In the fur country a man had to see in all directions at once, and to evaluate everything he saw without a moment's hesitation. When a man hesitated up in the country of the Blackfeet his scalp soon hung in an Indian lodge.

The hand holding the liquor glass was big and broad, and the fingers were short but not stubby. The back of the hand had a light covering of fuzz, the color of his hair and the color of his eyebrows. His shoulders were big, filling out the woolen coat that he wore in this cold spring weather. For a man who stood well over six feet in his socks he was not awkward, and he moved with the lightness of a panther, every bone and muscle coordinating.

His coat was open as he stood at the bar, and the bone handle of an Army pistol protruded from his belt, which was made of beads, the only concession he made to the old trapper's life.

He noticed that Jonas Keene and the little trapper in the fur cap were coming toward him along the bar, the tall, lean Jonas sliding in and out between men crowding up to the bar, moving the way he moved among the tall trees in the Northwest country, silent, mild brown eyes moving the way Scot's moved, always alert, the only thing alive in his smooth-shaven, brown face. Like Scot, he had acquired the Indian's taciturnity.

The little man with him was of the same breed, an older man, his buckskins blackened and shiny with grease, the fringes almost all worn off. He had a big hunting knife stuck in his belt, a buckskin sack for his possibles slung over his shoulder, and he carried his long rifle, a Hawkins gun, brass-mounted.

Jonas Keene said, "Jim Haggerty, Scot. This hoss just come in from Adams."

"How," Scot said. He pushed the bottle toward the two men, and Leon, behind him, put out two extra glasses on the bar.

"Heard o' you," Haggerty said. "On the Green River an' down in Taos an' a heap o' other places, MacGregor. Never run into you."

"You'll live," Scot murmured, and Haggerty grinned a little as he started to fish in his buckskin sack, coming out eventually with a small package wrapped in rabbit skin.

"Letter fer you," Haggerty said, "from a lady up at Fort Adams. Reckon you know who."

Jonas Keene said it for Scot. "Carole Du Bois," Jonas murmured, and the sound of that name stirred something in Scot's chest, something that had been lying dormant most of the winter.

"Red or white," Haggerty said, "damn if I ever seen more of a lady, MacGregor."

Scot just looked at him as he started to open the package, which had been sewn shut to keep out water and dampness as much as possible. The little mountain man seemed to realize that he had spoken out of turn, and he remained discreetly silent as Scot took the piece of paper from the package and unfolded it. Jonas Keene poured two drinks and handed one to Haggerty, and then both men leaned over the bar, speaking in low tones as Scot read the letter.

He'd known Carole could write, but he'd never before received a written message from her, and the sight of those small, well-shaped letters on the piece of white foolscap paper for some strange reason filled him with pleasure. Carole herself was like that, very neat, very clean, a mixture of the best of two races—the tall, handsome Cheyenne people and the France of Quebec.

Her mother had been a Cheyenne woman, and Scot had known her before she died of cholera, a beautiful woman, light of skin, with the eyes of a fawn, and still quite young when she'd died. Carole's father was the *engagé* for the Empire Fur Company at Fort Adams, the amiable, courteous Jacques Du Bois. Scot had known the family well since Carole was fourteen years old, and she was nineteen now, a tall girl with the dark hair of her mother and the blue eyes of her father. Every *voyageur* on the upper Missouri paid court to her, but she was still unmarried, and Scot had joked with her upon that subject many times as he sat on the counter in her father's store. Until last summer, however, he'd scarcely been aware of the fact that she was almost a grown woman, and no longer the little Indian girl for whom he brought presents from St. Louis.

Scot read the letter through slowly, a frown coming to his face, and then he read it through a second time before putting it into his pocket. Jonas Keene said over his shoulder:

"Bad news, Scot?"

"Jacques Du Bois is not well," Scot told him. "He's had the mountain fever, and Carole is worried."

Jonas shook his head in sympathy. "Not so good fer Carole," he said, "if Jacques kicks in, even if she is half red."

Scot didn't say anything to that, but he was thinking now of tiny Fort Adams, the Empire Fur Company post far up the Missouri. Jacques Du Bois was the only white man at the post. There were others—breeds who helped him, and always a dozen or two Indian lodges pitched nearby—and of the number a good many of them, red and half red alike, had cast longing eyes at the dark-haired Carole. If anything happened to her father she would be alone at the post, with the nearest white man back at Fort Tecumseh, over three hundred miles down-river. Fort Adams was in Indian country, too, bad Indians, Sioux and Assiniboins. So far Jacques Du Bois had been able to keep them friendly.

"Could be," Jonas Keene muttered, "Jacques has already gone under. Took Haggerty damn near a month an' a half to git down here from Adams by bull boat, an' then keelboat from Tecumseh.

Scot touched the little mountain man on the shoulder. He said, "How was Jacques Du Bois when you left?"

"He ain't looked good all winter," Haggerty said. "Had the fever in the fall, an' he's been in bed a lot."

"How about Carole?"

Jim Haggerty wiped his mouth with the back of his hand and started to fill his glass again. He looked at Scot carefully, and then said, "Reckon she looks all right to me."

The trouble was in Scot MacGregor's eyes as he slipped his hand into his pocket and felt the piece of paper there. Carole hadn't said it in so many words, but she was worried. She wanted him to bring medicines up from St. Louis, whatever the doctors thought would

14

help her father, and she wanted him to come quickly, if he could.

"Have to find that damned Baptiste tonight," Jonas growled, "or we'll go without him. Bad enough Brandon has that big lead on us, Scot. Now we got another reason for hurryin' like hell upriver."

Scot said to Leon, "Could be Baptiste is upstairs sleeping off a week's drunk?"

Léon shrugged. "*Mon Dieu!* Upstairs I never go, Monsieur MacGregor."

"I'll have a look," Scot said, and he pushed away from the bar, leaving Jonas Keene and Jim Haggerty to finish the bottle if they cared to. He placed a few coins on the wood to pay for it.

A dark-haired girl with liquid black eyes stood at the foot of the stairs, and she smiled and said, "Monsieur MacGregor." Her teeth flashed white, and her lips were very red. She wore a red dress that accentuated the color of her hair and her eyes.

"Baptiste Privot been in?" Scot asked.

A drunken Creole with a scarred ape's face came up behind her and put a hairy hand on her arm, trying to turn her.

"Peeg!" she snapped, and Scot MacGregor put his hand into the Creole's face and shoved. It did not seem to be a particularly hard push, but when the Creole hit the wall behind him there was a bang that could be heard the entire length of the room. His head snapped back against the wall, and he slid down slowly, staring vacantly.

The dark-haired girl put her hand on Scot's arm.

15

"Baptiste?" he said.

"I am not interes' in Baptiste," she said. "One more peeg."

Scot smiled faintly, lifted her hand from his arm, and started up the stairs.

" 'Nother peeg," she screamed after him.

Scot went up the stairs without even turning his head to look at her. He saw a boy sitting on the steps halfway to the top, looking down at the crowd on the floor below. The boy was about fourteen, pale, pinch-faced, his hat pulled low on his face, and he was shivering, his clothes wet from the rain. He had evidently just come in from outside, and he was sitting here where Leon and his bartenders would not see him and throw him out.

Pausing on the steps, Scot looked down at him. He said, "You have no home?"

The boy had deep black eyes. They were the eyes of a dog that had been beaten, and expected to be beaten again. He shook his head and Scot frowned. St. Louis was full of them—bond boys, boys who had run away from poverty-stricken homes, boys who wanted to see the Indians and the buffalo and trap beaver. He'd been such a boy himself, and he knew. He said, "When did you eat last?"

The boy's hands were clasped across his knees. He wore a short jacket, and his trousers were of hickory. The hat on his head was shapeless from the rain, the brim broken. The hands were slim and shapely, not the hands of a boy who had worked on a farm or who had done hard labor.

The boy murmured, "It was yesterday, monsieur. I

16

came up from Louisburg on the River Belle."

"Stowaway," Scot said. "You are from New Orleans?"

"*Oui,*" the boy said.

"And where do you go now?" Scot asked him, putting one big shoulder against the wall and looking down at him. Those small, shapely hands entranced him. He could not imagine what kind of work this boy would get in St. Louis. No apprentice would take him on. He had no strength in his hands or shoulders, which were slender.

The boy shrugged expressively, and he smiled a little, revealing small even white teeth.

"You were' better off in New Orleans," Scot told him. "At least it's warm there." He took a coin from his pocket, put it in the boy's hand, and went on up the stairs.

"*Merci bien,*" the boy called after him.

On the second floor landing Scot walked from door to door, looking into the rooms that Léon Lédéreaux rented as overnight lodgings. At this early hour of the evening he found but one of them occupied. A half-drunken keel boatman snored stentorously on one of the sagging cots in the nearly bare room. Baptiste Privot was not in the Red Lion.

Coming down the stairs again, Scot saw the boy sidling along the wall, heading for the door. He had his coat buttoned tight around his neck, and he was obviously trying to leave the tavern with as little notice as he had attracted when he came in.

The dark-haired girl with the red mouth was talking with a tall man in a frock coat, but she saw Scot as he went by, crossing toward the bar, and she stuck her tongue out at him.

Jonas Keene said when Scot came up, "No luck? This child's damn tired o' waitin' fer that Frenchie. Reckon we'd better sign up one o' these boys."

"On a two-thousand-mile trip that might take us three months," Scot observed, "a few days more or less won't matter. Baptiste is worth waiting for. He'll make up that time for us."

His wide face didn't show it, but Scot's patience was running out, and Carole's letter had made the the situation immeasurably worse. Already he pictured her up at the trading post alone, with the breeds eying her lasciviously.

Jonas Keene put his back to the bar and stared at the room. Haggerty was working on the bottle, and from the way he went at it, Scot could see that he'd be under a table in another hour. Jim Haggerty had a long thirst that had begun at Fort Tecumseh, seventeen hundred miles up the Big Muddy.

Scot glanced at Jonas Keene. Like Scot, Jonas had no use for the towns, and this prolonged delay galled him. Jonas had spent a dozen years in the big mountains; he'd been to the stinking springs and salt lake; he'd even gone as far as the Spanish settlements of southern California. He knew the West as few men knew it, and he preferred the solitude of the high mountains to anything the big cities could offer.

There was a livid scar across Jonas Keene's right eye where a Blackfoot arrow had creased him, and the scar seemed to pull the eyebrow upward, giving him a perpetual quizzical expression. He was lean and long with a thin face and lank brown hair to go with those mild brown eyes. He seldom smiled, and Scot never had seen him laugh.

Even in the towns Jonas preferred his buckskins to city clothes, and he'd worn them all winter while the Osage was being prepared for the long trip. When Scot left the mountains and the life of a free trapper to work for the Empire Fur Company, Jonas had gone with him, and was employed now as hunter for the company, providing fresh meat for the keelboat crews as they moved up and down the river.

Leaning back against the bar, watching the crowd, Scot noticed that the boy to whom he had given the coin was nearly to the door, reaching for it, when it burst open, the inward thrust knocking him back violently against a heavy-set man with a very red face and the rough clothes of a teamster.

The man coming through the doorway had shoulders that nearly touched each doorpost. He stood six feet, four inches in his stocking feet, and he weighed two hundred and thirty pounds. The Mackinaw made him seem even larger. There was a red woolen cap set back on his head, revealing his black, curly hair; his eyes were black, too, and gleaming with drink and good humor. On his upper lip was a small black mustache, pointed at the ends. His hands were the biggest hands Scot MacGregor had ever seen on a man, and the most powerful.

The giant stood there for a moment, grinning, swaying very slightly, his white teeth gleaming, the shine of liquor on his face, rain water glistening on his woolen cap and the tips of his curly black hair.

Scot heard Jonas Keene say softly:

"Baptiste Privot, you hairy ape!"

## Chapter Two

As Baptiste Privot stood in the doorway of the Red Lion, the boy whom he had knocked back into the room and against the teamster had recovered, and was now struggling to get to the door. The red-faced teamster, a big, heavy-shouldered man, almost as big as Baptiste, had him by the scruff of the neck and was shaking him violently, angered because he had been shoved.

Scot was pushing away from the bar to intervene when Baptiste Privot lunged forward, his wide brown face dark with wrath. Grabbing the teamster by the shoulder, he swung him around and rammed him back against the wall.

"*Sacrebleu!*" Baptiste growled. "You hurt the boy!"

The teamster, who evidently did not know Baptiste, thrust his arm away rudely and stepped away from the wall. He said, "Keep out of this, Frenchie, or you'll get that handsome face pushed in."

Big Baptiste stared at him for a moment, mouth open a little in amazement. "Me?" He gaped. "Baptiste Privot? Stronges' man in the Northwes'."

"You ain't in the Northwes' now," the teamster goaded. "You're in the good old United States—St. Louis, Missouri, an' there ain't a Frenchman from here to New Orleans kin stand up to Jack McGovern."

"Me," Baptiste boasted, "I will stand up, Monsieur Jack, and you will sit down." Jonas Keene chuckled. "This should be good, Scot. Baptiste's picked himself a big one this time."

"When Baptiste gets those big hands on a man," Scot said, "they're all small. Watch."

"That feller's got friends with him, too." Jonas nodded toward a group of other rough-looking men at the bar. "Maybe the big Frenchie's bit off more than he can chew."

"We'll see," Scot said.

Big Jack McGovern was rubbing his hands, and Scot saw him glance over toward the bar in the direction of the other teamsters with him. He grinned and said, "You want trouble, Frenchie, an' here it is."

He lashed out with his right fist, a full, clean swing, catching Baptiste Privot squarely on the jaw. There was a sickening spat, the sound of a rock being slammed down into a bed of mud.

Baptiste had his head a little forward when the blow landed, and he was an ideal target. He made no move to draw his head out of the way. He was grinning at the teamster as the fist came toward his jaw, and still grinning after it landed. The blow had about as much effect on him as if a butterfly had brushed a wing across his jaw in flight.

The teamster dropped his right hand, clutching it with the left, an expression of pained incredulity sliding across his face. He stared at Baptiste in amazement, and the big Frenchman whooped, "You want to play with Baptiste?"

21

"Hell, no," the teamster muttered, and then he was picked up bodily, Baptiste grasping him by the belt buckle and the shirt front, lifting him, and throwing him forward ten feet to land on a card table around which four men were sitting.

The table splintered as the teamster landed on it. Playing cards, drinking glasses, and players went down in a heap on the floor. The teamster rolled as he landed on the floor, put a knee on the chest of one of the card players, and rose to his feet, snatching up the broken leg of a chair.

Baptiste reached out with his huge hand and pulled a chair from beneath a card player at another table, dumping the player unceremoniously on the floor. He moved forward, laughing in rare good humor.

"Now," he boomed, "we play with sticks."

As he started forward, swinging the chair around as if it were a toy, one of the teamsters at the bar kicked another chair forward directly under Baptiste's legs.

The Frenchman roared in anger as he stumbled forward, off balance, and then Jack McGovern stepped up, grinning, and brought his chair leg down across Baptiste's red woolen cap.

The chair leg broke in two pieces, but Baptiste went down on hands and knees, stunned for a moment, looking around stupidly.

"All right," Scot MacGregor murmured, and he moved forward, Jonas Keene following, deftly sliding an empty liquor bottle from the bar, gripping it by the neck.

Four teamsters had moved from the bar to work on

Baptiste, and one of them was raising his boot to kick the giant in the ribs when Scot reached him.

Swinging the man around by the left shoulder, Scot crouched and rammed his right fist deep into the teamster's stomach, doubling him up and dropping him to the floor, out of the fight.

Jonas Keene grabbed one man by the coattails, yanked him back, and brought the liquor bottle down across his hat. The man sat down on the floor without a sound, the hat still on his head.

Baptiste, recovering quickly, was coming up off the floor as Scot went after another man. Jack McGovern had clambered over the broken table to get at Scot, but he never reached his man. Baptiste's big right hand moved out, the arm encircling McGovern's waist. Scooping the teamster back, he lifted him again, and this time slammed him straight down on the floor and stepped across him to get at another teamster.

The French Creole moved very swiftly now, like a great panther, sliding in front of Scot, reaching for the man Scot had been going after. The teamster cursed and slashed at Baptiste with both hands.

Baptiste brushed his hands aside, grasped him by both arms just below the elbows, lifted him, and slammed him back against the near wall. He held the man up on the wall two feet off the floor, and then as he let him slide, he swung his left fist—the short, effortless cuff of the big grizzly bear.

The teamster crumpled as the fist caught him on the chin. He fell to the floor like a dead man, and Baptiste Privot looked around for another victim.

One man remained out of the group of teamsters at the bar, and this man sprinted for the door, Jonas Keene's liquor bottle sailing through the air after him, crashing against the door lintel as the teamster lunged out into the night.

"Fight's over," Jonas murmured.

Baptiste Privot turned and looked at Scot. "*Mon compagnon!*" he whooped, and he threw his arms around Scot. "One, two, t'ree days I look for you, Monsieur MacGregor."

"Four days," Scot told him dryly, "and you weren't looking too hard, Baptiste: The Osage is waiting for you, and Brandon is damn near up to the Platte by now."

"We catch him," Baptiste said confidently. "*Mon Dieu!* Me, Baptiste Privot, best damn boss-man in Northwes'. We catch him."

He began to demonstrate how he handled the heavy pole up in the bow of a keelboat, warding off drifting trees and sawyers, lunging, poking, pushing with an imaginary pole.

Jonas Keene had drifted up behind Scot, and when Baptiste saw him he grabbed the lean man, drawing him close, kissing him on the cheek.

"My frien'!" he whooped.

"Hell with that," Jonas growled. "Come on back to the boat, you big ox."

"*Oui.*" Baptiste nodded. "T'ree days I have look for you.

"Where'd you think we had the Osage tied up," Jonas growled, "on somebody's rooftop?"

Scot put a hand through Baptiste's arm, leading him

24

toward the door, and for the first time he noticed that the boy who had been indirectly responsible for the fight had disappeared.

It was raining considerably harder now, the rain coming down in long, slanting lines, spattering the mud and the slippery boardwalk. Baptiste walked out into it, talking volubly as usual, gesticulating with both hands, entirely oblivious of the rain.

"T'ree day I have look for you," he said again to Scot.

"Under wine bottles," Jonas Keene said. "At the bottom o' liquor glasses. Snow'll be fallin' by the time we git up to the Trois Fourches, an' Brandon will have enough liquor in the Sioux so they'll be blastin' away at everything that moves on the river."

"Sioux?" Baptiste laughed. "Pouf! Blackfeet!" He grimaced, running a finger around his head in a scalping movement, and then grinned.

"You ain't tellin' me nothin," Jonas growled. "Had them devils on my tail many a day."

"Me, Baptiste," the French Creole was saying, "with naked hands I push them aside. With teeth—" He stopped speaking and he stopped on the walk, standing there in the rain, the yellow light from a nearby tavern lamp illuminating his face, dripping with rain. "Where is the boy?" he asked.

"The boy?" Scot said. "I guess he drifted when you went to work on the fellow in the Red Lion."

"Nice leetle boy," Baptiste said. "Pretty boy."

Scot found himself wondering about the boy, also, the boy with the slender girl's hands. On a night like this and out in the open it would be hard on a frail child. He wondered where the boy had come from and what would happen to him in this frontier town. With hands like that, he might have come from a good family—a good New Orleans family.

Back at the keelboat they went aboard, finding the crew, those of them whom Scot could not trust and whom he was afraid would desert, sleeping under lean-tos that had been stretched from the cargo-box out over the cleated runway for the polemen.

Aft of the cargo-box was a tiny cabin. They walked along the roof of the cargo-box, which extended almost the entire length of the boat, and then Scot dropped down to the deck, stooped, and entered the cabin, turning up a small oil lamp that burned there.

He located a few blankets for Baptiste, tossed them to him, and then let the Creole find a place for himself on deck.

The rain pelted down on the wood roof of the cabin and on the canvas tarpaulins. Sheets of rain swept across the river, a cold, chill April rain, and Scot found himself thinking about the boy again as he sat on one of the two low bunks in the room and pulled off his boots.

Jonas Keene occupied the other bunk as second in command on the boat. Scot, as bourgeois for the company, was captain and steersman. There were twenty crewmen, all French Creoles. Americans could not stand the grueling work on the runway or the cordelle line. They could not exist on the fare of lyed corn, salt pork, and beans, the steady diet until they reached the buffalo country.

Jonas said as he lay back on the bunk, "Glad we found

the big ape anyway, Scot. He's been drinkin' steady fer four days an' he don't show it any more than if he'd downed a half pint o' mild wine."

"Takes a lot of liquor to affect Baptiste," Scot agreed.

"Half a river," Jonas growled, "but I'm damn glad we got him, Scot. Might be we'll be needin' a few dependable men when we git upriver. Can't depend too much on this crowd. They're like ducks on the water; you git 'em off the river an' they're helpless, an' the Blackfeet have 'em all buffaloed."

Scot packed his pipe with tobacco, lifted the chimney from the lamp, and held the pipe to the flame, puffing on it until he had it going. He said idly, "You don't think much of this business, Jonas."

The lean hunter shrugged. "You know the Blackfoot country," he said. "You know the Blackfeet."

Scot looked at the lamp thoughtfully. "You know how important this trading post is, Jonas," he said, "and the posts the company will set up next spring."

"If we git through the winter," Jonas reminded him. He shook his head grimly. "Supposin' the government does git control o' the Oregon Territory. What in hell good is it? You bring settlers up there an' they'll die off like flies come the first freeze. Summer's too short an' winter's too tough. That's game country, Scot, not farm country."

"Other side of the mountains," Scot told him. "Down the Columbia. That's where the settlers will be going. Our posts will help them along. There won't be any of them stay in the Blackfoot country."

"Not if they want to keep the hair on their heads."

27

Jonas smiled. "You figure Brandon kin hurt us if he gits up to the Three Forks first?"

"He'll do all he can to influence the Blackfeet against us." Scot frowned. "Great Western Fur is out for profits. They're not interested in developing the country."

"They'd cut a man's throat fer a pack o' beaver," Jonas said, "but we got the government behind us, Scot."

"Government is in Washington," Scot observed. "Blackfoot country is not American and it's not British. Anything can happen up there."

"No man's land." Jonas scowled. "Fifteen hundred miles from nowhere. If we git rubbed out, who's to say it weren't the Blackfeet? That the way it looks to you, Scot?"

Scot nodded. "Brandon knows that, too," he said. "Upriver we'll have to set a double guard every night, and watch every bend of the river."

"Plenty to watch," Jonas murmured.

Scot puffed on his pipe and didn't say anything.

The rain had stopped in the morning, and a weak sun was trying to break through a wall of gray cloud. Scot checked on the Creoles aboard the keelboat, and then went ashore to round up the others who were bunking in nearby taverns.

An hour after dawn the men were at the long oars and the Osage had cast off ropes and was drifting out into the brown Missouri. The breeze was downriver, making the square sail useless this day.

Scot stood up on the roof of the cargo-box, holding the handle of the great sweep, guiding the Osage out into the river. Baptiste Privot, boss-man of the crew, stood up in the bow, long pole in his hands, swinging it about as if it were a light willow wand, ready to ward off drifting debris.

Jonas Keene sat on the roof of the cargo-box, staring upriver, his long rifle at his side. A chill, damp breeze swept downriver, and the tall hunter shivered a little. Looking back at Scot he said, "Set poles fer the Yellowstone, Scot."

Scot MacGregor nodded. They weren't using the long poles as yet because there was clear and deep water here, and the river was wide, but they were on the way, setting poles for the distant Yellowstone and the Blackfoot country.

A small crowd was watching from the levee as they moved out into the river. The Creoles broke into song, Baptiste Privot leading them in a bellowing voice. It was a song of the *voyageurs,* sung by men who had leaned into Indian paddles in years gone by, stroking their bark canoes up this same river, oftentimes with black-robed padres up in the bow, watching the riverbanks.

The big Missouri flowed down at them, brown and swollen with the silt of a thousand smaller streams oozing out of the vast Oregon Territory. Scot could feel the power of it as the twenty oars dipped into the water and the Creoles heaved against the current.

A faint cheer came up from the crowd on the levee, and then the Osage slid around a bend in the river and the town of St. Louis was behind them. Upriver were a few scattered Army posts—Leavenworth, Fort Tecumseh, Fort Union—and then nothing; a vast country of rivers and rolling hills and flat plains, and then the big mountains with the snow shining on their summits, and the dreaded Blackfeet trapping the beaver streams and watching for the white hunters, whom they hated and whom they fought with a ferocity not surpassed on the American continent.

The keelboat handled well, and she was a good boat, a new boat constructed downriver. Eighty feet long, with the cargo-box and small cabin taking up almost the entire length of the boat, and with the big hickory mast set up in the bow, she was built for Missouri service, propelled by brute strength.

The broad-backed French Creoles were the engines to make her go. They rowed, they poled with the long poles, they manipulated the sail; and when these methods did not work, they went over the side with the thousand-foot-long cordelle line, stumbled, crawled, and scrambled through mud, swamp, and sometimes river water up to the shoulders, dragging the line, and then hauling the boat upriver, pulling in the line hand over hand.

A small brass cannon up in the bow of the Osage caught the faint gleam of the sun. It was a little four-pounder, mounted on a swivel, ready to sweep either bank, and it was a gun the Indians dreaded even though the damage from it was considerably less than might be expected from the noise and flash of fire when she went off.

The brown hills closed in around them as they left St. Louis. Along the banks willow, cottonwood, and small oak were bursting into leaf, showing light green against the darker hills beyond.

Scot took the keelboat up along the east bank, close in to the shore to avoid the strong current. The smell of the river came to him, clean and fresh, and he breathed deeply, getting the fetid city air of out of his lungs.

At high noon they pulled in to the west bank. Romaine, the cook, got his fire going, his pots over the fire, and the beans and salt pork in the pots.

The Osage had been snubbed against the bank, willow branches hanging out over the bow. The sun was still weak, with very little warmth in it, and gray clouds were driving downriver. Jonas Keene had gone upriver with his rifle when they touched the bank, and he came down now with the smell of hot coffee in the air. He said to Scot, "Company comin' in fer dinner. Pirogue."

Scot walked down to the water's edge to look out over the river. He could hear the faint slap of oars, and then the pirogue slid around a bend of the river, two men at the oars, heading in toward the keelboat. A third man sat in the bow of the boat, and he lifted a hand to them as he caught sight of them on the bank.

"Comin' down from Leavenworth," Jonas Keene said. "They might have some news from upriver."

The two men at the oars were Creoles, stolid, brown-faced men with immense shoulders. The man in the bow was an American in faded buckskins with a slouch hat. He was not a big man as he stood up, rather slender in the shoulders, clean-shaven, his face lean and brown.

He was smiling as the pirogue put in to the shore, passing around the bow of the Osage. When he stepped ashore, small, trim, blue-eyed, he came toward Scot and

31

Jonas, hand outstretched, smiling. "Lucien Weatherby, gentlemen, at your service."

Scot heard Jonas Keene say softly, "Damned Injun painter!"

There was respect and admiration in the hunter's voice, and Jonas Keene did not admire or respect too many people.

Scot gripped the small man's hand. "Heard about you, Weatherby," he said. "Coffee's on the fire."

Everyone on the Western frontier knew of the fabulous Lucien Weatherby, the artist, who in canoe, pirogue, bullboat, and on foot traversed the upper Missouri River basin, sketching and painting Indians. Even the mountain men had their respect for this fearless little man who could walk boldly into a Sioux or Assiniboin village, set up his easel, and begin to work. His Indian paintings were internationally known, and even though he could have long ago retired on the money they had brought him, he preferred the life on the big plains and in the high mountains, making his sketches, daily risking his life, living alone, hunting and traveling with the mountain men, visiting tribes with whom even the mountain men were unfamiliar.

By strange coincidence, Scot had never run across Weatherby, although he had heard countless tales of the man. He had expected an older man, but Weatherby was probably not much older than himself, and he had reached his twenty-ninth birthday this winter in St. Louis.

"Heard the Osage was headed upriver," Weatherby was saying. "Came down from Leavenworth to meet you, MacGregor."

32

He had small, shapely features, the palest blue eyes Scot had ever seen, almost doll's eyes, but they looked straight at a man, and they did not waver. His hands were small as Baptiste Privot's were huge. They were slim, brown, and shapely, and for a moment Scot was reminded of the hands of the boy in the Red Lion, except that there was strength in Lucien Weatherby's hands.

Weatherby was clean-shaven, his nut-brown hair cropped short under the flat-crowned hat he wore. As he squatted on the ground Indian fashion and accepted the plate of beans and salt pork that Romaine handed to him, he thanked the cook politely as if he were sitting in a New Orleans restaurant.

The two crewmen with him had joined the Osage's crew, and Scot could hear their laughter behind him, light and rippling like a mountain stream as they spoke in rapid French, and he conjectured that they were discussing their last visit to the Ree village upriver, and the Ree squaws they'd met.

Weatherby had the voice of an Easterner, Scot judged the Maryland or north Virginia country, a very slight Southern accent. He was a cultured man with background and education, and he spoke like one. He said, "Been talk along the river that Empire Fur intends to set up a trading post deep in Blackfoot country."

Scot nodded. "Our stick points that way," he admitted.

Lucien Weatherby inclined his head slightly as he looked down at the beans and pork and then started to eat. "Dangerous country," he said. "You know that."

"I know it." Scot smiled.

"I have never painted the Piegan Blackfeet," Weatherby went on. "I have come downriver with the intention of joining up with you, if you would have me. I shall, of course, pay my fare."

"We'll pay you to come along," Scot told him. "Empire Fur spent all winter trying to line up a crew for this trip. Not too many volunteers to go up to the Blackfoot country."

Weatherby looked up from his plate. "I am obliged," he said simply.

Scot scratched on the ground with the point of a stick. "You passed the Yellowstone Gal on the way downriver, Weatherby," he said.

Weatherby nodded, no particular expression on his face.

"Reckon she's headed the same way we are," Scot went on.

Weatherby looked at him over the rim of his tin coffee cup. "I've met Cass Brandon," he said, "and I've heard of Scot MacGregor. I prefer the Osage if I have my choice."

"You have the choice." Scot smiled at him.

An hour later the pirogue was headed downriver again with the two Creoles at the oars, and Lucien Weatherby sat on the cargo-box of the Osage, ready to spell Scot at the handle of the sweep.

In the late afternoon the wind changed and the Missouri made one of its tortuous swerves. Scot ordered the sail up when he felt the breeze on his back, and the oarsmen rested on the deck as the square sail billowed and the keelboat moved crisply upriver.

Scot said to Weatherby, "How far ahead is Brandon?"

"He has four days on you, but this is a fast boat. You'll catch him above Leavenworth." He paused, looked at the west bank of the river and the distant hills with the sun dropping behind them, coming out strong now at the end of the day, and he said, "Are you looking for trouble from Brandon?"

Scot shrugged. "Two rival fur boats on the Missouri," he stated. "It's always a race to the fur grounds, and no holds barred."

"Not with Brandon in the other boat, anyway." Weatherby nodded. At the sweep he guided the Osage around a big cottonwood that had been torn from the banks a thousand miles upstream by the fierce current, and was still drifting just above St. Louis.

With the long pole Baptist Privot poked at some branches of the tree that scraped along the bow of the Osage, and then they were clear, sailing north and west on the river.

At dusk they pulled in to the east bank, tying up in a cove. They'd made good time the first day, aided by that upriver breeze. The Creoles were in good humor, having rested all afternoon, and they wrestled and joked while Romaine got the cook fire going and the beans in the pot.

"Won't be this much play," Jonas murmured, "when they been out all day in the rain with the cordelle line. Be glad to flop in their blankets an' call it quits."

The night closed in around them, and the stars peeped out among the trees surrounding the cove. A crescent moon slid up above the rim of hills and a nighthawk screamed faintly upriver. Frogs along the banks croaked hoarsely, and a fish leaped in the cove, making a splashing sound as it struck the water again.

Scot placed his tin plate and cup on a rock near the fire, watched the Creoles rolling into their blankets, saw Jonas Keene begin to stuff his clay pipe, and then he walked down to the bank. The Osage lay not more than fifteen yards from him in the water, a rope running out to the bow and tied to a tree on the bank. There was no current here in the cove, and the keelboat lay motionless in the still water.

Taking his pipe from his pocket, Scot opened his tobacco pouch, and it was then that he saw the faint movement on board the deserted boat. He stood motionless, watching, knowing definitely that they had left no one on board the boat, and thinking that perhaps it had been a shadow caused by the moon.

As he watched he saw movement again aft of the cargo-box, a shadow stealing forward along the starboard side, and he remembered that while this was not Indian country, they had enemies on the river—enemies who would be very happy to see the Osage destroyed before it got upriver with its valuable cargo of trade goods.

## Chapter Three

Walking back to the fire, Scot squatted down next to Jonas Keene, who had his pipe going and was warming himself near the fire. He said, "All the crew accounted for here, Jonas?"

Even as he said it his eyes were moving around the

camp, counting the men—Romaine, Baptiste Privot, Garand, Le Beau . . . He went down the list, and Jonas Keene said, "What's up, Scot?"

"Somebody on board the Osage," Scot told him. He finished his count of the crew, Lucien Weatherby watching him from the other side of the fire.

Jonas Keene got up lazily. "I'll go aboard at the stern," he said, and he picked up his blanket and moved back into the shadows as if he intended to find a place to sleep for the night.

Scot poured himself another cup of coffee from the pot, and as he was doing so he said to Weatherby, "We have a visitor on board. Going out to have a look at him."

Weatherby lifted his eyebrows slightly. "Brandon?" he asked.

Scot shrugged. "He could have left a few men behind, waiting in a canoe, to board us some night."

Finishing the coffee, he put the cup down and tossed a few sticks on the fire. Then he moved out of the firelight as if searching for more wood, and he noticed that Weatherby had gotten up also and walked over to his pack to look through it.

When Scot was beyond the firelight, under the trees along the edge of the cove, Weatherby joined him, and then big Baptiste Privot loomed up behind Weatherby, having sensed the fact that something was wrong.

When Scot told him briefly, Baptiste swore under his breath.

"If they put the fire to the Osage," he muttered, "I will cut out their heart."

"Jonas is going aboard at the stern," Scot told them. "We'll walk out and climb aboard up in the bow."

"You saw only one?" Weatherby asked.

"May have been more," Scot said. "You have a gun?"

Weatherby nodded.

"We'll swing out wide around the cove," Scot said, "and approach the boat from the bow. They'd see us coming straight at them from the camp."

"*Mon Dieu.*" Baptiste scowled. "One night out from St. Louis."

Circling the cove, they stepped into the shallow water when they were about thirty yards from the bow of the Osage, and started to move forward slowly. The water came almost up to their waists when they came in under the bow, circled, and hauled themselves up to the deck.

They lay there dripping water for a few moments. Scot was crawling over to the cargo-box when they heard the sudden movement in the stern. Footsteps sounded on the runway, and Jonas Keene yelled, "Grab him!"

Baptiste Privot lunged ahead of Scot, and as a dark figure ran toward them, Baptiste's huge arms encircled it. There was a brief struggle on the runway, and then Baptiste started to laugh softly deep down in his chest.

"I have a gun on him," Scot said. "Disarm him and bring him ashore, Baptiste."

"*Oui.*" Baptiste chuckled. "This is one good catch, *mon compagnon.*"

Jonas Keene came down the catwalk to say, "Only one of 'em aboard, Scot. Ain't seen a boat of any kind. He must have waded out."

"This one," Baptiste grinned, "he walks without touching water."

Lucien Weatherby said, "Stowaway, Scot."

Jonas Keene, who could see like a cat in the dark, had stepped closer to Baptiste Privot. He said briefly, "It's that damned boy we saw in the Red Lion, Scot."

Scot shook his head in disgust. "Take him ashore, Baptiste," he ordered. To Lucien Weatherby he said, "Another one wants to see the West. He must have sneaked aboard last night and hid inside the cargo-box."

Baptiste Privot had gone over the side, and he had the boy slung over his right shoulder as he started toward the camp on the shore. The crew had come down to the shoreline to stare at them stupidly. Baptiste was still chuckling as he waded through the water, and Jonas Keene, coming after him, said sourly, "What in hell's so funny, Baptiste? We got our breeches wet account o' this damn fool boy."

"This boy," Baptiste said, "is one nice boy." Then he slapped the boy on the rump with his big hand, and he laughed uproariously as the boy on his shoulder wriggled frantically to get loose.

As they came up out of the water and into the firelight, Scot said, "We'll drop him off at Leavenworth. We can't afford to go back to St. Louis now."

He watched Baptiste set the boy down on the ground, and the boy turned to look at him, shoulders turned inward, face pinched. He'd probably had nothing to eat since he'd come aboard the Osage, and he'd been searching for food when Scot had seen him.

39

"This one," Baptiste said, "the Army will not take, *mon compagnon.*"

"They don't have to take him," Scot said. "We'll just leave him there until a boat can take him back to St. Louis."

Baptiste was still grinning. "One nice boy," he said, and then he pointed at the boy and roared with laughter. *"C'est une fille!"*

Scot heard Jonas Keene gasp, and then he stepped forward and took the hat from the boy's head. The hair was cropped short and dark, and it was very full. With the hat off he had a better look at the face also, the small features, the small, slightly upturned nose, perfectly shaped mouth, the dark, soft fawn's eyes.

"A girl," Jonas Keene muttered.

The Creoles, forming a semicircle around them, were staring too, open-mouthed, at the boy who had turned out to be a very pretty girl.

Scot MacGregor's mouth was tight. He ordered the crewmen back to the fire and took the girl by the arm, leading her to a seat on a box near the fire. Romaine ladled out a platterful of beans and salt pork, and Scot poured a cup of coffee. He said, "Eat," and then he put a coal in his pipe and puffed on it furiously.

Lucien Weatherby was watching him from across the fire, a faint smile of amusement on his brown face. He said eventually, "Quite a surprise, Scot. What are you going to do with her?"

Scot scowled again and shook his head. He watched the girl eating hungrily. When he looked at her she smiled back at him, revealing small, white teeth. He said rather gruffly, "What is your name, mademoiselle?"

She was of French extraction. She had the features, the coloring, the dark eyes of a New Orleans woman.

"Nanette La Rue," she said.

"What are you doing on board my boat?"

The girl shrugged, another typical French gesture, and she raised her eyebrows slightly. "I have no place to go, and I was wet and hungry, monsieur. You were kind to me in the Red Lion."

"What were you doing in St. Louis?" Scot asked her.

"Do you have any folks?"

"*Non,*" she said.

"You came up from New Orleans," Scot growled, "dressed as a boy so that you could travel alone. Were you a stowaway on the steamer, also?"

"*Oui.*"

"And what were you looking for in St. Louis? Why did you come?"

"I am looking for a nice, good man," Nanette La Rue said simply, and she looked straight at him.

Scot MacGregor felt the color come to his face. He heard Lucien Weatherby chuckle softly, and even Jonas Keene was grinning from his seat on the other side of the fire.

"Men are few and far between in this part of the country," Scot said. "You should have stayed in New Orleans, or even in St. Louis."

"I need but one man, monsieur," she answered and smiled at him.

"An' you're elected, Scot." Jonas Keene grinned.

"We'll drop you off at Leavenworth," Scot told her.

41

"I'll pay your passage back to St. Louis. We can't turn back now."

"*Non*," she said.

Scot looked at her in exasperation. "You can't go up river with us. That's Indian country. There are no white women up the Missouri."

"I will be one," Nanette La Rue said simply. "I will cook. I will clean your cabin."

Scot looked at Lucien Weatherby, who was smiling broadly.

"She might have enough of it by the time we reach Leavenworth," Weatherby observed.

"I'm thinkin' not," Jonas Keene said.

Scot puffed on the pipe moodily. He said to the girl, "You'll sleep in the cabin on board. There will be no men on the boat any night."

"I do not wish to take your cabin, Monsieur Mac-Gregor," she protested.

Scot looked around the campfire at the Creoles, who were squatting on the ground, saying nothing, their dark eyes shining.

"You'd better go aboard," he said dryly. To Baptiste Privot he said, "You will carry the mademoiselle aboard, Baptiste, and see to it that no one goes near the boat when we camp at night."

Baptiste grinned. "I will cut off the ears and the nose of anyone who will touch the lady. Understand?" He glared around the campfire at the men and they looked away uneasily.

When Baptiste picked up Nanette La Rue, shifting her easily to his broad shoulder, she smiled down at Scot.

42

"*Bon soir,*" she said.

"Good night," Scot nodded. He watched Baptiste wade out into the water with her, and then he saw a crack of light on board the Osage as the lamp in the cabin was lighted, and then Baptiste came back to the shore, water streaming from his legs.

Jonas Keene said as if reading Scot's mind, "Reckon we have some trade goods in the cargo-box, Scot. She could make herself a skirt an' blouse."

Scot nodded. "She can't wear that outfit," he said.

Baptiste Privot stood by the fire like a huge dog having just come out of the water. He grinned at Scot and said, "The lady wants a man."

"You're a man," Scot said.

Baptiste shook his head and his grin broadened. "No, no," he chuckled. "You, *mon compagnon.*"

Scot frowned, and Jonas Keene said blandly, "Kind o' got yourself fouled up, ain't you, Scot? Allus figured Carole Du Bois was waitin' fer you upriver."

"Carole could have a man by this time," Scot told him.

"She wanted a man," Jonas said, "an' she could o' had fifty since she was sixteen years old, an' you know it."

Scot didn't say anything to that. Looking out over the cove at the Osage, Scot saw the crack of light around the small cabin door, inside of which Nanette La Rue was making herself at home. He considered the small, boyish Nanette, who very definitely had informed him that she liked his company. There was no Indian blood in Nanette, and to some men that would have made a difference. Scot was sure it did not to him, but he watched the crack of light until it disappeared before he rolled into his blanket.

43

## Chapter Four

Nanette La Rue made a pretty picture in her bright red skirt and white blouse as she stood on the roof of the cargo-box, the wind catching at the skirt, her dark hair, beginning to grow long again, ruffling in the breeze. She had made the skirt and blouse out of trade goods that had been intended for Blackfeet squaws, and had proved very adept with the needle and thread.

When she had stepped out of the cabin two days after they discovered her on board the Osage, even Lucien Weatherby had looked at her with interest as he worked on one of his Indian sketches on the lee side of the cargo-box. The skirt and blouse fitted her well, and the bright color of the skirt matched the smooth olive complexion and the dark eyes, flashing with laughter and good humor.

Scot, standing at the sweep, watched her for a moment as she stood there, legs braced against the wind. The Creoles were on the runway, long, steel-tipped poles in hand. The current was strong here and the wind downriver. Scot had taken the Osage in close to the shore, where the poles could touch bottom, and the men had been at them for over an hour now as they worked slowly upriver, yard by yard.

"*A bas les perches!*" Scot shouted.

The men lowered the poles into the brown water, feeling for the bottom, and when they had it, they drove forward, the balls of the poles in the hollows of their shoulders, clawing for the cleats on the catwalk, bending with the strain of their drive.

On both sides of the cargo-box the men surged forward, gasping with the effort as they drove the poles into the river bottom. The keelboat slid forward, and when the first man in line reached the end of the catwalk, he straightened up.

*"Fort!"* Scot called sharply. *"Levez les perches."*

The two lines of broad-backed, brown-faced men in wool caps and cloth coats straightened, swung about, and hurried forward.

*"A bas les perches,"* Scot MacGregor yelled.

They caught her before the current stopped the forward drive, and then pushed and strained forward, step by step, dark eyes bulging, lips parted, teeth clenched from the strain.

Baptiste Privot, whirling his long pole up in the bow, shouted and cursed at them, urging them on to greater efforts as he poked his pole at drifting debris.

Scot watched a brown lump slide by on the starboard side—a drowned buffalo from far upriver, bloated, only the hump showing. Nanette La Rue pointed at the dark shape in the water, and Scot nodded. She smiled at him, flashing white teeth.

As they moved slowly around a bend in the river, Scot saw a dead deer hanging from a limb out on a point, and then far upriver he heard a rifle crack. Jonas Keene was up there along the shore, ranging ahead of the Osage, bringing down an occasional deer, and ducks or geese.

Turning the keelboat in toward the shore, they picked up the deer, then they moved out again, the men still at the poles and the low brown hills closing around them.

45

"*Levez les perches,*" Scot ordered.

Poles lowered, the Creoles strained, and they gained a few more precious yards on the river. Ahead lay the Sister Islands, a trio of green islets through which the brown current surged with too much force even for the poles.

Turning in toward the bank, Scot ordered the crew out with the cordelle line, and reluctantly they went over the side into cold water up to the waist, struggled to shore with the thousand-foot line, and then started up along the bank, stumbling and sloshing through mud and willows, dragging the line several hundred yards until it became taut.

With Baptiste Privot holding the Osage away from the shore with his pole, the men started to pull in the rope hand over hand, drawing it slowly up along the bank past the first and then the second islands until they had hauled it the entire length of the line.

A loop was drawn around a tree on the bank, securing the Osage there, and then the men moved forward again, dragging the cordelle line another thousand feet through brush, over creeks with the water coming up to the shoulders; and then the hard haul again, and a few more hundred yards gained on the Big Muddy.

It was slow, hard work, even more uncomfortable than at the poles, where at least the men could keep dry while they worked. Here they struggled along the bank like so many dogs, slipping and falling in the mud, fighting their way through willow and brush and brier, always wet through to the skin, cursing the branches that slapped at their faces, cursing the long, heavy line they had to drag.

Jonas Keene came aboard with a brace of Canada geese after the second haul, and he said succinctly, "Hell of a river, Scot. Here's hopin' we git an upriver breeze when we pass Leavenworth. Be all summer an' half the winter reachin' the Great Falls."

Scot watched the Creoles clamber over driftwood along the bank, every once in a while one of them falling off a slippery log, splashing in the river, and getting up, spluttering, cursing, to drag the line.

Beyond the Sister Islands they were able to use the oars again. Lucien Weatherby took the sweep, and Scot had a few words with Nanette La Rue. He said as he sat on the edge of the cargo-box. "We will be at Fort Leavenworth tomorrow. That will be the end of the trip for you, Nanette."

"*Non.*"

Scot looked at her, exasperation in his face. "We can't take a woman with us to the upper river."

"There is a woman up there, I am told. Mademoiselle Carole Du Bois."

"She is part Indian," Scot explained. "She was born at Fort Adams on the upper river."

"I am born on the lower river. I want to see the upper river."

"You must go back to St. Louis," Scot said grimly.

"I will scream." Nanette smiled at him. "I will screech like an Indian. I will tell men that I am your wife and that you are sending me away."

"You're *crazy*," Scot muttered.

Her voice turned to pleading. "I have nothing at Leavenworth," she said. "Nothing at St. Louis. Nothing in

New Orleans. I must go with the Osage."

Scot looked over at Jonas Keene, sprawled on the cargo-box roof behind him, and then he shook his head in disgust. Daily he'd had this argument with Nanette La Rue, trying to convince her that she had to turn back at Leavenworth, and daily she'd pleaded that he let her remain on board.

He had to admit, however, that her arguments were good. She had no friends in St. Louis, and if she had to return there it would be to walk the streets and to beg, or worse.

Even Jonas had conceded that Nanette had an argument. At least on board the Osage she had friends, and she'd made herself useful, helping Romaine at the cook fire each night, mending Scot's clothes.

"Lookin' at it from her side," Jonas had stated, "it would be a hell of a deal to send her back, Scot."

"You can't take a white woman upriver," Scot growled, "with twenty-five men aboard. We'll be on the water several months. We'll winter upriver."

Jonas just shrugged. "Baptiste will look after her," he said.

Scot had learned a little more of her past during the days they were moving up the Missouri. She told him that her father had had a small shop in New Orleans, a bakery shop. When he died there had been a little money, a very little, and then when it had been used, she'd slipped on board a Mississippi steamer as a stowaway, taking boat to Louisburg, and then to St. Louis.

She had no relatives—in France, perhaps, but not in America.

48

"Why did you come north?" Scot had wanted to know.

"I did not like New Orleans," Nanette had said simply, and that was the end of it. She did not seem to be particularly worried about her situation, as long as she could stay on board the Osage.

Nanette sat next to him on the roof of the cargo-box, looking very small. She said, "If you send me back to St. Louis, I will do very bad things. You understand?"

"You're crazy," Scot muttered.

"*Oui,*" Nanette agreed, "but I must eat. It is not pleasant to starve to death."

"You can work as a maid in one of the rich homes," Scot told her.

"*Non,*" she said. "I do not like rich homes and rich men. Rather would I walk the streets and talk to men, and—"

"That's enough," Scot snapped. He said no more on the subject.

At high noon the next day the Osage turned in toward Fort Leavenworth on the Missouri. The fort was built on a series of bluffs overlooking the river. Outside the walls were a scattering of houses, a landing dock for boats, and a few Indian tepees, probably Osage or Delaware.

Scot went ashore to secure his trading permit, and a government agent checked on the cargo of whisky aboard. Each keelboat moving upriver was checked for whisky to see that the traders were not selling hard liquor to the Indians. A bourgeois was permitted only enough whisky for his crew—a gill a day for each crewman for four months.

Before going ashore Scot looked into the cabin and

saw Nanette La Rue under the blankets on one of the bunks. "I am not going, monsieur," she said.

"We will be here two days," Scot told her. "Talk about it tomorrow."

"I am not dress," Nanette said.

"Where are your clothes?" Scot asked her.

"In the river."

"You will have them on tomorrow.

"*Non.*"

Scot went ashore with Lucien Weatherby and Jonas Keene. The Creoles also went ashore, and Scot saw them prowling among the Indian tepees, looking for likely squaws. There weren't too many squaws, however, mostly older women and children.

"They'll have better luck," Jonas observed, "when we reach the Ree villages up above Fort Tecumseh."

Securing the permit at headquarters, the three of them stopped in the sutler's store for a drink, and they were still there at dusk, chatting with a few officers who had come in, hearing the news of the upper river, when they heard the shouting down at the water's edge.

They took no particular notice of it, thinking it was likely a fight between one of the Creoles and a townsman or soldier, and Scot was stuffing his pipe when they heard the dreaded cry:

"Fire! Fire on the Osage!"

Shoving his pipe in his pocket, Scot leaped toward the door, beating Jonas Keene out by one step. A sharp breeze had sprung up from the north, whipping down-river. The Osage lay a hundred yards away from them, down the graded road to the dock. They could see the flames breaking out at the forward end of the cargo-box.

Men were running in all directions, shouting, calling for buckets. A bucket line was already being formed as Scot tore through the crowd, tumbling men to either side. He heard Jonas Keene say behind him, "Nanette's still aboard, Scot."

Scot hadn't forgotten about the French girl in the cabin, pretending that she'd thrown her clothes over-board. When he crossed the plank he headed toward the stern and the cabin. Smoke drifted toward him, choking him. He noted that only the forepart of the cargo-box was burning; the flames had not yet reached back to the middle or rear sections.

"Git them axes in the cabin," Jonas whooped.

Running down the cleated runway, Scot bumped full into someone coming the other way—someone small and soft. He had a glimpse of Nanette La Rue's face in the reddish light of the flames. He noticed that she was wearing the boy's clothes she had had on when first he'd seen her. Her face was wild, tears from the smoke trick-ling down her cheeks.

"Get over the plank to shore," Scot ordered, and then he gave her a push toward the plank and went on to the cabin. Snatching two axes from the locker inside, he handed one to Jonas, and they raced back to hack at the cargo-box, chopping away the burning timbers and kicking them into the river.

A bucket brigade, with Lucien Weatherby giving the orders, had finally been formed, and water started to come toward them, Weatherby tossing it over the flames, passing his empty bucket back, snatching another from the man behind him.

"Ain't too bad," Jonas yelled. "First compartment on fire. We got to it on time."

An unending stream of water came aboard the boat, and Weatherby continued to slosh the buckets full into the cargo-box until the last spark had been put out.

Scot kicked over a few charred boards, the siding of the cargo-box, listened to them hiss as they hit the water. He said briefly, "Bring a few lanterns here. We'll see the damage."

"Ain't too bad," Jonas Keene repeated. "Another few minutes an' we might o' lost this boat."

"There was no fire on board when we came ashore this afternoon," Scot said. "Anybody besides Nanette aboard?"

Jonas shook his head.

"I should have known better than to leave the Osage unguarded," Scot growled, "even in town."

"None of us figured on trouble at an Army post," Jonas told him. "Reckon we'll know better the next time."

"Nanette give the warning of the fire?" Scot asked some of the nearest crewmen standing by.

"Sentinel up at the post saw the flames," a man told him. "Gave the warnin'."

Lucien Weatherby came out of the shadows up near the bow as lanterns were being brought from the cabin. The artist said, "Have a look at this, Scot."

Scot followed him up into the bow. Weatherby had secured a lantern, and he held it up and leaned out over the bow. A hawser line had held the Osage to the dock.

The line had been hacked with an ax or a knife, and was nearly cut through. A single strand held the keelboat to the dock.

Scot looked at Weatherby. He said briefly, "Another rope runs out from the stern."

They went back along the catwalk to have a look at the stern line, and found it cut through, the rope now hanging limp. Scot called for Baptiste Privot to secure new lines. He said to Weatherby, "If that thin strand had parted, the Osage would have drifted out into the river. When the full wind caught it the fire would have spread in less than a minute. We'd have lost our boat."

Weatherby nodded. "Who do you think?" he asked.

Scot MacGregor's mouth was a thin straight line. "Only one man on this river wants to see the Osage stopped," he said "We know who that is. They lost out when they failed to cut through that line."

"Nanette may have seen someone," Weatherby said.

Scot went ashore as the crewmen, under the light of lanterns, chopped away the burned and charred timbers so that the carpenters could go to work in the morning on the repairs to the cargo-box. The damage had not been particularly great. Some cartons of trade blankets had been burned, but a good many of the blankets could be salvaged.

Nanette La Rue was standing on the little wooden wharf when Scot crossed the planks. She came toward him immediately. She was hatless, and she smelled of smoke. He wondered why she'd put on the boy's clothes again, and then he realized that if she'd smelled fire it was more logical to wear these clothes rather than a skirt

53

or dress, which would catch fire more easily.

"What happened?" Scot asked her.

"I heard the flames," Nanette told him, "and then the smoke came into the cabin. I put on my clothes and I run. I try to fight the fire. I call for help."

"You see anyone?" Scot asked her.

"*Oui.*" She nodded immediately. "One man run from the bow along the runway. Then I hear canoe paddles. They go upriver."

"They drifted down on the Osage," Scot growled, "boarding her from the river side. You did not see the man's face?"

"*Non,*" Nanette said regretfully.

"They came from upriver," Scot said, his hands tight at his sides. "We know who is upriver."

"I do not understand," Nanette said.

"You'll know someday," Scot told her. Cass Brandon would know, too, when they caught up with him. He made that pledge.

## Chapter Five

In two days they had the cargo-box repaired and repainted and were ready to go, and still Scot hadn't made up his mind concerning Nanette La Rue. He'd spoken with her at long length the morning after the fire, pointing out the dangers of an upper-river trip, and the fact that they would not be coming downriver in the fall as most keelboats did. It meant a long winter at a lonely trading post with the feared Blackfeet all around them, and only the hope that they would be able to keep the Indians in good humor.

"You will not come back?" Nanette asked thoughtfully.

"No." Scot shook his head. "I will stay upriver. The Osage will return in the spring, but I will stay at the post. Other boats will be coming up next summer to establish more trading posts."

"Then there will be more people," Nanette said, "more women?"

"No more women," Scot told her.

"*Non?*" Nanette smiled mischievously. "That is good. Then I will go."

"You'll stay," Scot growled, "if I have to hog-tie you and leave you on the dock when we cast off."

Nanette looked at him pleadingly. "You will have me walk the streets with the bad men?" she asked.

"Rather that," Scot snapped, "than to have your hair hanging in a Blackfoot lodge."

Nanette nodded soberly. "You are worried for me," she said, "and that is good. I will not go all the way with you."

"All the way?" Scot repeated.

Nanette turned to him. "You will stop at Fort Adams," she said, "and there is a woman at Adams, and a sick man. You understand?"

"No."

"I will stay at Fort Adams with the other woman," Nanette smiled happily, "and I will help her with the sick man. In the spring I will go back with the boat. I will not go to the country of the Blackfeet."

Scot saw Jonas Keene nodding his head as if she'd hit

55

upon the solution. He didn't like the idea of sending Nanette back to St. Louis, penniless and homeless. At least at Fort Adams she would be taken care of, and she could be of help to Carole in tending her sick father.

"You will take me?" Nanette clapped her hands happily.

Scot looked at Jonas again, and then he nodded. "As far as Adams," he said. "Reckon you'll be safe enough there. We'll leave some of our crew at the post when we go on."

Nanette threw her arms around him, held him tight, and kissed him full on the mouth.

"That's enough," Scot growled. He disengaged her arms, but even as he did so he was conscious of a vague reluctance to break the contact. She was a woman, a very pretty one, and she would be aboard his boat for a long time, the only woman in this part of the country with the exception of Carole at Adams. He wondered how that was going to work out on this long, slow voyage upriver, and he almost began to regret that he'd given her permission to come along.

It was too late now, however, to change his mind. Nanette was dancing around on the roof of the cargo-box, singing happily. He did not have the heart to spoil it.

Jonas Keene said, "If you're worried about the crew, Scot, Baptiste kin take care o' them. They won't go near her."

Scot nodded. Ironically, he had to admit to himself that it wasn't just the crew he was worried about.

The Osage slipped away from Leavenworth the day

after the fire, the men at the oars pulling lustily, Baptiste Privot leading them in song, and Nanette cheering from the cargo-box roof.

An hour after losing sight of the Army post they hit an upriver breeze, and Scot ordered the sail raised. For two hours then they moved along at a spanking pace, the men resting on the deck, happy for the respite; but in the afternoon the breeze dropped, the river narrowed, and the men picked up their poles.

"*A bas les perches,*" Scot called.

It was poles and then the cordelle line until dusk, when the men stumbled into camp, wet, disgruntled, having been softened in their few days' stay at Leavenworth.

Scot ordered Nanette on board the boat soon after eating, and she went without a word, the men looking after her as she crossed the plank that had been stretched out to shore.

When the men rolled into their blankets, Scot sat by the fire with Jonas Keene and Lucien Weatherby. He watched Weatherby finishing out a sketch of a Mandan Indian. He had begun the sketch upriver with a living model, and now he was filling in the details from memory.

They could hear the water slapping softly against the bow of the Osage as she rocked gently on the hawser lines. A nighthawk screamed downriver, and then they heard a coyote off in the hills. The river had opened up here, the big plains extending in all directions as far as the eye could see, and Jonas Keene had stated in a few days he would be bringing in buffalo treat. Both banks of the Missouri were still tree-lined and the islands had their covering of vegetation, but beyond lay the grass-lands, an unending blanket of short buffalo grass.

Jonas Keene said, "Might catch up with Brandon sooner than we think."

"He's been moving," Scot commented, "while we've been held up at Leavenworth."

"Could o' run into an *embarras,*" Jonas pointed out. "Damn river's full of 'em farther up. I've seen a keel-boat spend a week tryin' to git through." He added, "Seen keelboats lost, too, in the attempt."

"We can't lose this one," Scot said. "It's more than just a cargo."

Lucien Weatherby, who knew of the Empire Fur Company plans, nodded soberly. "About time steps were taken to consolidate this territory," he stated. "British fur companies have been up here for years, but they don't encourage settlements. They want to keep it wild so that it will produce fur."

"United States government wants to open it up," Scot explained. "You've been on the other side of the mountains, along the Columbia and the Willamette. You've seen that rich, black soil."

Lucien Weatherby nodded again. "There's a pass up in the Flathead country. In ten years you'll see wagons going through there by the hundred once word gets out about that soil. The land's free for the asking. It'll draw them by the thousands from the fever-infested Missis-sippi Valley and farther east."

"Be plenty o' hair hangin' in the Blackfeet lodges, too," Jonas Keene said.

"Our forts might make friendly Indians out of the

Blackfeet," Scot said. "That's one of the purposes of our trip."

"Only friendly Blackfeet I know," Jonas grunted, "are dead an' buried."

For five days the Osage moved steadily upriver, by pole, by cordelle line, by oar, and by wind. It was slow, backbreaking progress. Once when the water was too deep inshore for the poles, the current strong, and the wind in the opposite direction, the Creoles stood on the catwalk and propelled the Osage forward by grasping overhead branches.

They stood in waist-deep water at other times, dragging the keelboat forward, and always they moved upriver, with the giant Baptiste Privot cursing, threatening them, cajoling them. His booming voice reached upriver when they were hauling the cordelle line through swamp and willow, sliding and scrambling over sand bars in water that was still very cold. He sang as they handled the oars, and they kept time with the beat of the old *voyageurs'* songs. Always he was in the bow with his heavy pole, swinging it about, poking it, occasionally leaning far down to thrust aside with his bare hands the branches of a half-drowned tree.

Lucien Weatherby said to Scot once, "That man's worth a half dozen of the best crew I've ever seen on this river."

"Reckon we gained three-four days on Brandon," Jonas Keene said. "This crew is movin' along, Scot."

One noon they came upon Brandon's campfire of the previous night, the ashes still warm, and Jonas kicked it thoughtfully.

59

"Tomorrow," he said.

Scot set a double guard that night, putting two men on board the keelboat also, to prevent anyone from climbing aboard from the river side. He had done this since leaving Leavenworth, and the first night away from the fort Baptiste Privot had crept on board to find one of the guards outside Nanette's cabin door. He'd tossed the man ten feet out into the river with the threat that he would cut his throat or the throat of any other man who came within ten feet of the door on any subsequent night.

After that Scot ceased to worry about the girl. Nanette slept on board. She was happy and carefree during the day, making herself useful in many small ways, and Scot tried not to think about the future. It was one day at a time up the Missouri—a day of rain and wet clothes and misery till the evening campfire, and then a day of sunshine with the heat coming into the sun, and the men beginning to sweat at the poles, and to discard some of their clothing.

Late afternoon of the next day they saw the keelboat Yellowstone Gal tied up at the head of an island known as Cow Island. Wood smoke curled lazily up through the trees on the east bank of the river, and Scot, at the sweep of the Osage, could see men moving about on the shore.

Baptiste Privot shouted back, "*Embarras!*"

Scot saw the water tumbling down through a chute between the island and the west bank. Floating debris, giant trees, sawyers, silt, and even dead animals had choked the regular channel through which keelboats moved past Cow Island. The water tumbled through a

60

narrow passageway, white, foaming water, a passageway not more than twenty feet wide.

Cass Brandon had pulled up here to figure out a way to get past the *embarras.* It was going to be dangerous. Scot MacGregor had ascertained that before he swung the tiller handle and sent the Osage in toward Brandon's camp.

Jonas Keene sprawled on the roof just looked at him and spat a straw out of his mouth. Scot called to Nanette La Rue, who was just coming out of the cabin. He said, "You will remain inside the cabin while we're tied up here, Nanette. I don't want Brandon's crew to see you."

"*Oui.*" Nanette nodded. "They are bad men."

The Creoles were at the oars, pulling in toward the shore, all of them aware of the fact that there was going to be trouble, and looking up at Scot uneasily. If he'd wanted to avoid trouble he would have tied up on the opposite bank instead of taking the Osage to within a few yards of the Yellowstone Gal.

When they were within thirty yards of the bank Scot saw Brandon come down to the water's edge and watch them. Brandon's yellow hair caught the last rays of the falling sun. He was big, bigger than Scot, but not as big as Baptiste Privot. He wore a checked woolen shirt, and he stood with his heavy arms on his hips, grinning at them.

One winter Scot had trapped beaver with this man in the Jackson Hole country, and he'd seen enough of him not to want to associate with him again. There was much he hadn't liked about Brandon. It was the way he killed an injured beaver, the way he treated a squaw, the way he rode a horse. There was an animal ferocity in the man concealed by a cold blandness, and it had taken Scot months to discover it. Brandon liked to see others hurt, to watch them squirm.

In the four years since they'd trapped together Brandon had become bourgeois for the Great Western Fur Company, a cutthroat outfit that existed largely because of the whisky it traded to the upper-river Indians.

Baptiste Privot went over the side with the hawser line when they were within fifteen yards of the shore. Another line from the stern was wrapped around a tree on the bank, and the Osage was securely tied.

Scot touched tinder to a Spanish cigar, checked the hawser lines, and then went ashore. Jonas Keene said as he went down the plank, "Easy, Scot."

The hunter trailed behind, his long rifle in the hollow of his arm. They walked through the bushes toward Brandon's camp, fifteen yards away, and when they came out into the clearing they saw Brandon seated on a rock in front of his cook fire.

He was a handsome man, clean-shaven, with solid jaws and light, whitish eyebrows to go with that pale hair. His eyes were green and slanted a little. His hands were big, broad, short-fingered, powerful. He was grinning, revealing strong white teeth.

"How," he said.

Scot stopped on the other side of the fire. "*Embarras* stop you, Brandon?" he asked.

"Go through it in the morning," Brandon told him. He was still grinning as if at some secret joke. "You made good time, MacGregor," he said.

"Had a little trouble back at Leavenworth," Scot said, "or we'd have been past you by now."

Cass Brandon lifted his white eyebrows in mock concern. "Trouble?" he repeated.

"Some skunk tried to burn us out," Scot said. "Stink of his own fire drove him off."

Brandon wasn't smiling any more. The Creoles with him, a tough, scarred, burly crew, watched him, the whites of their eyes showing. The fire crackled between Scot and Cass Brandon. Scot saw Lucien Weatherby coming through the bushes, and he noticed that Weatherby had a pistol in his belt, and he knew why Weatherby had come. He and Jonas Keene had sensed a fight, and they were there to see that their bourgeois got a fair deal.

There would be a fight, too. Scot had known that from the moment he'd seen the Yellowstone Gal tied up on the shore, and even farther back, when they'd seen the Great Western campfire still smoldering. Brandon had fired the Osage, and he was sitting here gloating over the trouble he'd caused. If he weren't stopped now he would become more bold farther upriver. A man like Brandon thrived on another's timidity.

Brandon said tersely, "Don't come around here cryin' over your troubles, MacGregor."

"Figured you might know something about it."

"How?"

Scot shrugged. "We didn't see the varmint. Slunk off too quick. But I had a look at his hair. You wearing a hat four-five nights ago, Brandon?"

Cass Brandon stood up. "You talk," he said, "like a man who came here itchin' for a fight."

"Never ran away from one," Scot observed.

"You never had one," Brandon smiled, "like the one you're runnin' into now, MacGregor. Get the hell out of this camp."

"Shores of the Missouri are free land," Scot said. "I stand where I damn please."

He watched Brandon coming around the fire, and he noticed that the Creoles had started to breathe more heavily. Some of his own men were sifting through the bushes, forming a semicircle around the Brandon camp. Big Baptiste Privot stood in the fore, staring at Brandon's crew contemptuously.

"Me, Baptiste, he boomed, "with the bare hands I tear away the *embarras*. With the teeth I have kill the mountain bear. *Mon Dieu,* is there not one man here who will play with Baptiste?"

There was no response from the Brandon crew. They knew Baptiste. They'd watched him in fights in St. Louis and upriver. He was stronger than a grizzly, and the most skilled fighter in the Northwest with his feet.

Cass Brandon stopped within five feet of Scot, looking him over, and Scot was thinking of the times when he'd shared a mountain cabin with this man.

"You won't leave peaceable?" Brandon said.

Scot just smiled back at him. He said nothing, but he remained where he was, hands at his sides, waiting, remembering that Brandon too was adept at the art of feet fighting, having learned it from the French Canadians.

He was ready, then, watching Brandon's feet more than his hands, when Brandon suddenly leaped forward, kicking with his right foot at Scot's face. Scot saw the foot coming up and he pulled back. The boot, if it had landed, would have literally kicked Scot's mouth in.

Brandon spun gracefully, making a small arc, and came down on hands and feet like a big cat.

"*Sacrebleu!*" Baptiste Privot roared.

"Stay out of it," Scot called without looking at the big crewman.

Cass Brandon straightened up, smiling, looked at Scot's face, and then kicked savagely at his right knee. Again Scot pulled back, the boot grazing his leg. This time he didn't remain back. Driving in, he lashed at Brandon with both fists, forcing him backward, and then he leaped to one side as Brandon aimed another vicious kick at him.

Blood started to trickle from the blond man's cut cheek as he straightened up. He knew then that he had to fight this one American style. They stared at each other warily, and then Brandon circled, came to a stop, and leaped in, lashing out with his right fist. He moved with incredible speed for a man of his bulk, and the blow caught Scot on the side of the head, knocking him to the ground.

Brandon was on top of him in a moment, slashing at Scot's face, trying to drive his knee into Scot's chest. Rolling desperately, Scot threw him off, hitting him a jolting blow in the mouth as he scrambled away.

For a moment Brandon squatted on hands and knees, blood spouting from his lacerated mouth, and then he got up. He kicked experimentally, and then leaped in, trying to grapple Scot around the waist and throw him to the ground.

Scot came up hard with his knee into the blond man's face, and he heard the bones of the nose crack. Brandon let out a short, stifled grunt of pain as he staggered back, and then Scot was on top of him, striking hard, stiff blows to the body as Brandon covered his face with his hands.

The circle of yelling Creoles from both boats opened as the two fighters lunged through, Brandon with blood streaming from his broken nose, trying to steady himself and fight back. He was still dangerous, still capable of turning the tide of battle, and Scot knew it.

Brandon went down, rolled and got up, the blood smeared all over the lower part of his face now. As Scot leaped in at him to finish the fight, Brandon started a blow with his fist, and then kicked out with his right boot instead, catching Scot full in the stomach.

Gagging, clutching at his stomach with both hands, Scot pitched forward, twisting his head to one side as the grinning Brandon aimed another kick, this time at his mouth. Had the boot landed it would have driven all of Scot's front teeth to the back of his throat. The tip of the boot grazed Scot's jaw as he turned his head instinctively, and then he lunged forward on his knees, grabbing Brandon's legs with both arms, knowing that he had to hold those deadly boots now or be terribly disfigured the remainder of his life.

Brandon cursed and beat him on top of the head with his fists as he tried to break loose. With Scot pushing against him Brandon lost his balance and crashed back to the ground, still kicking with his knees and beating at Scot's head with his fists.

Desperately Scot hung on, rolling with him. He felt Brandon's hands tearing at his hair, trying to push his head back so that he could get at the eyes. His breath and his strength were beginning to come back now, and he knew if he could hold on a few moments longer he would be all right.

Brandon had managed to get one leg free at last, and as they rolled on the ground, he again kicked savagely. Without looking at him, Scot suddenly poked a fist straight up into Brandon's smashed nose, and the blond man let out a scream of pain, rolling away into the bushes.

Rising to his feet, Scot waited for him, his breath coming in long, hard gasps. Tears of pain were streaming down Brandon's cheeks as he finally righted himself and came up to the fight, but this time Scot had recovered.

"Git him now," Jonas Keene growled.

Scot moved in low, hitting from a crouching position, watching Brandon's legs carefully. That hard thrust up to Brandon's nose had taken much of the fight out of him. He kicked several times, tried to punch, and then Scot hit him several hard blows to the face and he sat down on the ground, shaking his head. He waved Scot away, and the fight was over.

Without a word, Scot turned and walked back to his camp, his crew following him, cheering lustily. Nanette was looking over the roof of the cargo-box when he came back to their own campfire, and Scot waved her back.

Lucien Weatherby poured Scot a cup of coffee and handed it to him. He said, "A good fight, Scot."

Scot shrugged. He walked down to the river to wash his bruised knuckles in the water, and when he came back Weatherby said, "Hate to have to fight a man who used his feet like that. I've seen men nearly killed and their faces pulverized from that French style of fighting."

"Not pretty," Scot agreed. "Knew a Frenchman at a trappers' rendezvous up on the Gallatin. Taught me how to fight them."

"You've made an enemy," Weatherby observed, nodding toward the Brandon camp.

"I've had one," Scot said dryly, "since we left St. Louis. Now it's out in the open where I want it."

"How important is it for Brandon to beat you upriver?" Weatherby wanted to know.

"First keelboat upriver," Scot told him, "picks up all the prime furs from Indian trappers. Second boat gets what's left. I've seen keelboats dragged eighteen hundred miles up to the Yellowstone, a whole summer to do it, and come back with a loss because another boat had beaten them to it. Men like Brandon will even bribe Sioux and other tribes to attack the boat behind them to make sure it won't beat them to the fur grounds."

"Is Brandon going up into Blackfoot country, too?"

"That was the talk back in St. Louis," Scot said. "He knows it's dangerous, but he's loaded down with whisky for trade."

"Against the law," Weatherby murmured. "How did he get it past Leavenworth?"

Scot shrugged. "False compartment in his cargo-box," he said. "Or he could move it upriver at night in a pirogue or two, and then pick up the kegs out of sight of the fort the next day. There are many ways, and Cass Brandon knows them all."

"That hoss is smart," Jonas Keene admitted.

"I'd watch him from now on," Lucien Weatherby said.

"We ain't forgettin' about him," Jonas Keene said. "Too much at stake this trip to let a dog like that ruin it."

Scot MacGregor was thinking the same thing. There was too much at stake—possibly a vast territory that one day would be American, or part of British Canada. History often hinged upon smaller freaks of chance, or the evil of a single man.

## Chapter Six

In the morning Scot crossed the river with Jonas Keene in the painter to have a look at the channel and the *embarras*. Cow Island choked up most of the river with the passageway up along the west bank of the mainland. The debris had piled up against the island, extending farther and farther out into the stream, choking it so that now only a twenty-foot passageway remained close in to the shore.

One huge cottonwood had become lodged between the island and a rock, the dead branches protruding out into the channel. Against this single tree other drifting trees had piled—cedar and dwarf piñon from far up the river.

The debris had piled up so tightly that it was possible to walk about on it. The river tumbled around the far end of the *embarras,* white, foamy, the current much too strong for poling, too narrow for the oars, which left only the cordelle line, and even this was dangerous in that strong current. It had stopped Cass Brandon temporarily.

A dozen or more drowned buffalo floated or were wedged into the mass, making the air stink round about. Crows and other birds of carrion hovered above the odoriferous mass, wheeling and dropping to rise again into the air.

"Only thing," Jonas Keene said, "is the line, an' it's gonna be one hell of a pull fer them boys. You figure that mast will hold it, Scot?"

Scot nodded. "Hickory mast," he said. "If we can keep the bow straight into the current every moment we should make it."

"Why do you figure Brandon ain't tried it already?"

Scot shrugged. He'd thought of that, too, but had no answer for it. Brandon was not a particularly cautious man, and there had been no reason for him to stop here when the cordelle line was the only way for them to get by the *embarras.*

"Reckon he wants to see if we drown ourselves, first," Jonas said and grinned, "an' he ain't got Baptiste Privot up in the bow with a pole."

When they rowed back to the keelboat the crew were having breakfast on the shore. Scot pulled himself up on the keelboat to see how Nanette was doing. There were two guards on board the Osage, both with rifles, and with strict orders to let no one aboard.

A short, squat Creole by the name of Gaston squatted near the plank that extended to dry land. He looked at Scot uneasily when Scot came aboard and walked back toward the cabin.

A few minutes later Scot came back to the plank, his face grim. He said, "Where did she go, Gaston?"

Gaston's brown eyes rolled. He scratched his chin and hitched his shoulders. "*Parbleu!*" he muttered. "She go ashore."

"I told her not to," Scot snapped.

"I no understand."

"You understood damn well," Scot retorted. He went across the plank, telling himself that he was a fool for permitting Nanette to go along. There would be trouble if any of Brandon's crew spotted her in the woods. There would always be trouble with a girl aboard, especially as pretty a girl as Nanette La Rue.

Lucien Weatherby was just coming back into camp. He had some of his sketching paper under his arm, and Scot presumed he'd gone downriver to sketch some bird he'd seen the day before.

"Seen Nanette?" Scot asked him.

Weatherby's brown eyes lifted. "She's not aboard?"

"Walked right down the plank," Scot said in disgust. "They didn't know she was supposed to remain on board. "They knew, but Nanette smiled at them."

"She can do it with that smile." Weatherby grinned.

Scot found Baptiste Privot at the fire, gulping down a steaming cup of black coffee.

"Nanette came ashore," Scot told him. "You seen her, Baptiste?"

71

Baptiste looked around. "*Mon Dieu!*" he muttered. "Where would she go?"

The camp had been set back twenty-five yards from the shore on higher ground, and Nanette easily could have come down the plank without being seen at the camp, but why she'd come ashore and where she'd gone Scot could not imagine. Very possibly, however, she resented being confined to the cabin.

Jonas Keene said from the other side of the fire, "Comin' in now. Looks like she's been walkin' in the woods this mornin'."

Scot turned to watch Nanette walking toward the fire, coming around a clump of cedar beyond the camp. She was wearing the boy's jacket and trousers and a wool cap she'd borrowed from one of the Creoles.

"*Bon jour*," she said cheerily as she came up to the fire.

"You were told to remain on board," Scot told her grimly.

"Pouf!" She laughed. "They do not see me. I walk in the woods."

"Why?" Scot scowled.

"I am tired of boat. Always boat."

"You wanted to come aboard."

"*Oui*," she agreed. She looked at Scot beseechingly. "Do not be angry, *mon compagnon*. I am tired of boat. I go for walk in morning when Monsieur Brandon's crew is having breakfas'. They do not see me. I am small boy."

She looked down at the pants, and then up at Scot, and smiled again, revealing small, white teeth. Her dark eyes were pleading.

72

"All right," Scot growled. "Eat your breakfast and get back on board. We're leaving in an hour. If any of Brandon's crew drift over this way, you leave immediately."

"*Oui.*" She laughed.

"Just tired of the cabin." Weatherby smiled when Nanette went over to the cook fire.

Scot nodded. The odd thought came to him that Nanette had never gone walking in the woods before, and it was strange that she should do so now. He attributed it to her natural frivolity. She was as lighthearted and as careless as a kitten, acting on the whim of the moment.

Weatherby said, "You are going past the *embarras* today, Scot?"

"Aim to," Scot told him.

"Brandon's still in camp," Weatherby observed, nodding toward the other campfire a short distance up along the shore. "It appears to me that he's waiting to see what you will do."

"Have to move," Scot said. "That *embarras* will be there until the big floods break it up."

"The cordelle line?" Weatherby asked.

Scot nodded.

When they finished breakfast, they broke camp, and without a word to Brandon or his crew in the other camp, they rowed the Osage across the river, tying up on the opposite bank.

Scot had a look at the channel, studying it from every angle, Baptiste Privot at his side. It was about a hundred and fifty feet long, half again the length of the Osage, before they hit quiet water, but those hundred and fifty feet could be the death of the keelboat.

"Have to keep her nose straight into it, Baptiste," Scot said. "If the current swings us around and hits us broadside, the Osage will go over."

Baptiste nodded. For once he wasn't smiling. The river could carry them to where they wanted to go, and it could destroy them. It was at the same time a friend and a foe, and it had its moods like a woman.

"All right," Scot said.

"Reckon I'll go up with the boys along the shore," Jonas Keene said as he dragged the heavy coil of rope from under the tarpaulin in the bow. "Give us the sign when you're ready to pull," Scot told him. To Lucien Weatherby he said, "Can you handle the sweep, Weatherby? I'll be up in the bow with Baptiste. It'll take two of us with poles to keep her steady."

"Right," Weatherby said.

The crew splashed over the side with the line, waded to shore, and then started up along the bank. A hitch had been taken around a tree on the bank, and Baptiste worked easily with his pole, pushing the Osage away from the bank, but still not out into the swift current.

Weatherby went up on the roof of the cargo-box to take the handle of the sweep, and Scot picked up an extra pole. He saw Nanette La Rue watching them from shore, still dressed in the boy's clothes. He'd ordered her ashore, leaving only Baptiste, Weatherby, and himself on board the Osage in case she did go over. Nanette was to join them with the crew up beyond the *embarras*.

Across the river Brandon and his crew watched from

the shore, making no sounds. Cass Brandon stood a little to one side, hands on his hips, hatless, the bright morning sun on his blond hair.

Waiting with his long pole in his hand, Scot watched the crew scramble up along the shore, dragging the line. The brown water surged against the dam, foaming as it swung around the tip of the mass, and then tore through the channel.

The cordelle line lifted out of the water, dripping, as the Creoles drew it taut less than a hundred yards upstream. Scot looked at Baptiste Privot, and then at Lucien Weatherby up on the box behind him. Weatherby nodded that he was ready.

Scot watched Jonas Keene upriver with the crew. Jonas had a hand on the line too, and as the men braced themselves on the slippery bank, the hunter took off his hat and waved it.

Scot lifted a hand to Nanette La Rue on the shore a dozen yards away, and Nanette stepped to the tree and slipped the hitch, letting the Osage run free.

"Now," Scot muttered.

The crew had started to pull in the line attached to the mast. The cordelle line tautened, coming up out of the water. Scot and Baptiste poled hard, pushing the Osage out into the current.

They were moving now as the crew pulled her in, and they were heading out into the current up toward the passageway.

Scot felt the strength of that water as it hit them. The Osage shuddered, and Baptiste grunted as his pole bent. Scot dug down into the river bottom with his pole, holding her steady. He didn't look back at Weatherby any more; they could not relax for one moment now. If the river turned the Osage's bow even the slightest degree and she started to swing, it might be all over.

They were a dozen yards from the beginning of the *embarras* now, the foaming water driving out of the channel, smashing at them. Scot smelled the rotting buffalos in the water. He was conscious of the birds wheeling about overhead in the cloudless sky. When the bow of the Osage started to swing in his direction he dug in frantically with his pole, exerting every ounce of strength, and with the crew pulling on the line, straightened her out again.

When the pull was on Baptiste's side, he stopped poling, or he scrambled over to help, and they kept her steady in the channel, moving slowly, almost imperceptibly, the mast arched from the terrible strain on it, and Scot prayed that the mast wouldn't go. He wasn't afraid of the line. He'd personally purchased and inspected that line back in St. Louis. It was the best rope available.

The Creoles pulled the Osage in as if it were a huge fish. They hauled the line in hand over hand, slipping and slipping on the bank, digging in for leverage with Jonas Keene roaring at them.

The keelboat was inside the channel now, the brown water surging past on either side, making a roaring, hissing sound.

"Steady!" Scot shouted.

The Osage began to swing a little like a kite on the end of a string, edging toward his side, and Baptiste lunged over with his pole and dug it into the river bottom, stopping the sway.

Scot could hear Jonas Keene's sharp voice now as they drew nearer, already halfway past the *embarras* with open water beyond. The horrible thought came to him that if a sawyer or submerged log suddenly ripped into this channel from above, all would be lost. They had to hope that in these five or ten minutes the channel would be clear.

He was conscious of the fact that Nanette was running up along the bank, keeping abreast of the Osage, but he didn't look at her. He watched the water, and the bow of the keelboat, and the rocks along the shore, and the dead branches of the huge cottonwood that had been the foundation of this *embarras,* reaching out to grab at them as they went by. He watched everything and he felt everything, and he thought of a whole winter's planning and preparation back in St. Louis, of conferences in the office of the Empire Fur Company, of earnest government men consulting with them, poring over maps of the Oregon Territory, making dots where the line of posts would go, and where the settlers with their wagons and goods would follow.

He remembered tramping the wet, muddied streets of St. Louis, entering innumerable taverns, talking with the Creoles, trying to persuade them to sign up, and seeing the fear in their eyes when he had to mention that they were going up into Blackfoot country.

All of it now hinged on these few remaining minutes as the crewmen hauled in the Osage, fighting a whole mad river, a big brown devil of a river—a river that killed buffalos and men and keelboats, that tore giant trees from the banks as if they were willow shoots and whirled them a thousand miles downstream as if they were feathers floating on the surface.

"*Mon Dieu!*" Baptiste Privot gasped once. "We are almos' through."

The bow of the Osage was reaching now for the head of the *ernbarras;* inch by inch, foot by foot, she moved on. The hot morning sun beat down on them. Sweat poured down Scot's face, and he was scarcely conscious of it until it got into his eyes and he could not see well.

He could see the Creoles now, straining on the bank, bent almost to the ground with the effort. The long line of men strained and reached forward and pulled in another yard of line.

Scot had his pole in the water, straining on it, holding the Osage steady, when the line of men went down. It was almost laughable to see them fall. One moment they'd all been on their feet—twenty-one of them, holding on to the cordelle line—and then suddenly they were sprawled on the ground, holding a loose end of rope in their hands. It was as if they were tenpins and all of them had been swept from standing positions by the heavy wooden ball.

Baptiste Privot whooped in anguish, and Scot saw the cordelle line disappear in the water where it had broken.

## Chapter Seven

The cordelle line sagged down into the water, the strong current swinging it around on the port side of the boat. His pole braced on the river bottom, trying to keep the bow of the Osage directly into the current, Scot MacGregor watched the line sliding past him in the water. That line was more than a piece of rope attached to a keelboat at one end and loose at the other. It represented something. It was man's fight against the river; it was one nation against another, striving for a vast territory. The Osage wrecked this spring could mean the end of America's chances of consolidating the territory of the Northwest. If the British line of forts came down from Canada, the Oregon Territory would become a crown possession.

Lucien Weatherby, up on the cargo-box, trying desperately to keep the nose of the keelboat into the current, shouted, "Scot! No!"

Scot was already over the side. It was only three feet from the catwalk to the water. As he lunged downward, head first, he reached for that trailing rope, one hand tightening about it as his body went under the foaming water.

When he came up, shaking the water from his face, he saw the Osage's bow being forced toward the right bank of the channel. The current was forcing them rapidly back through the channel up which they'd come a few moments before. Baptiste Privot worked like a madman with the big pole, leaping from one side of the boat to the other, whooping, digging his pole into the river mud, trying to keep the bow pointed upriver so that the current couldn't hit it broadside. Lucien Weatherby was clinging to the tiller handle, staggering like a drunken man, striving to hold his ground. He went down on his knees, bent over the sweep, holding it steady.

Scot with the rope in his hand was tumbled over and over in the water. The rocky shore of the channel was less than a dozen feet away. In calm water he could have made the distance with a few powerful strokes, but it was impossible to swim here.

The water was suffocating, twisting him around, whirling him over and over when he tried to make headway, and it was difficult swimming with the rope in his right hand. Above the roar of the river he could hear Jonas Keene shouting at him, and he had a glimpse of the tall hunter sprinting down along the bank toward him. He had to get that rope end to shore so that Jonas could loop it around a tree and hold the Osage steady in the treacherous channel.

As he hurled himself through the water he was conscious of the fact that the Osage was sliding past him, the current driving it hard now. The rocks along the shore were very close, almost within reaching distance. As he lunged forward, reaching for the nearest rock, the foaming water rolled him again. He felt his back strike something hard behind him, driving him up against it, and when he reached with his free hand, his face underwater, he came in contact with the rough and slimy surface of a log that had become lodged among the rocks here.

He got an arm around the log, pressing his face against it, and then he swung his other arm over the top of the log and heaved himself up out of the water.

With the Osage still sliding rapidly back through the channel, it would only be a matter of moments before the rope in his hand became taut. Stumbling up over the rocks, the rope in his hand, he saw Jonas Keene leaping through the willows toward him.

Exhausted, Scot went down on hands and knees just as Jonas snatched the rope from his hand and made two quick loops around a four-inch cottonwood sapling on the shore.

The small tree bent as the rope tightened and the Osage came to a stop in the channel. On deck Scot saw Baptiste Privot leaping from side to side with his pole, desperately striving to keep the nose pointed upriver. Before, he'd been working with Baptiste, and they'd scarcely succeeded. Now the giant boss-man had to do it alone.

The dazed Creoles who had been hauling on the cordelle line were standing up now, staring down at them. Jonas Keene roared, "Here! Bring that rope. Romaine—the rope!"

Scot rose to his feet, river water streaming from him. The Creoles were coming down along the shore, yelling, dragging the rope with them.

Jonas Keene, watching Baptiste up in the bow, said dully, "He'll never hold her, Scot."

The Osage was whipping from side to side. Lucien Weatherby still clung to the sweep handle. As the Osage's nose started to point toward the island shore, Baptiste Privot dug his long pole in on that side, and the pole bent with the terrific effort, but the Osage came around again.

The Creoles scrambled through the willows with the rope, and Jonas rapidly tied together the two loose ends. They started up along the shore again, dragging the rope, Jonas Keene leading them. Scot remained behind at the sapling to slip the hitch when they'd drawn the line taut. He watched Baptiste with the pole, noticing that the giant was beginning to waver now as he lumbered back and forth to either side of the deck, but still the Osage's bow pointed upriver.

Jonas Keene was shouting from the point upriver where the crew had fallen when the rope parted. Scot stepped to the sapling, slipped the hitch, and watched the rope whip out into the water. He ran upriver himself then, passing Nanette La Rue, who had been watching from a distance, horrified.

He joined the crewmen and they started to pull in the Osage again, moving it inch by inch and foot by foot up through the channel. Scot watched the tall mast sag again under the terrific strain. He saw Baptiste stumbling back and forth with his pole, going down on his knees once, getting up again to drive the steel tip of the pole into the banks.

"Might make her now," Jonas Keene panted behind Scot.

All of them were on the line, hauling in the boat, digging in with their heels, straining, the rope lifting out of the river. The crewmen slipped, got to their feet again, cursing, pulling, the rope burning their hands.

They drew her in hand over hand up to the mouth of the channel, and then out of the fast-running water. Head sagging, Baptiste Privot poled the boat in toward the shore in quiet water. He was sitting on the deck, head down, shoulders heaving, when Scot pulled himself over the side.

The Osage was securely tied to the bank. Lucien Weatherby came off the cargo-box, rubbing his hands, the strain still in his face. He shook his head at Scot and said, "A rough passage."

Scot put a hand on big Baptiste's shoulder, slapped it in appreciation, and then opened one of the lockers to get out the brandy. He gave the jug first to Baptiste, still sitting on the deck, and the giant nodded, taking a long draught before rising to his feet.

The brandy was then sent ashore to the crewmen, and as the jug was going the rounds Jonas Keene signaled for Scot to come ashore also.

Nanette was coming aboard across the plank that had been thrown to the shore. She looked at Scot and she said simply, "I am so glad your boat was not wreck."

"We're all glad," Scot told her. "We're resting up here for an hour, and you'd better keep out of sight in case Brandon's boat comes through."

Nanette nodded obediently and stepped into the cabin.

On shore Jonas Keene led Scot through the bushes, following the line of the cordelle which had been carelessly pulled up on the shore and dropped when the Osage came out of the channel.

When they came to the point where the rope had been parted, Jonas squatted down on his haunches. He said, "Have a look at them ends, Scot."

Scot bent down to pick up one of the loose ends of rope. He examined the other end also, and then he said one word: "Cut."

The hunter nodded, his mouth tight. "She was cut

halfway through," he said. "Damn line broke when the strain came to it."

Scot stood up, dropping the rope. He put his back against a tree and stood there, arms folded across his chest. His face was expressionless, but a pulse began to beat in his right temple.

"As far as we know," he said, "no one got aboard the Osage last night. We had a double guard posted."

"You know what that means," Jonas said.

Scot nodded. "One of the crew works for Brandon."

"Which one?"

Scot looked at him, and then looked away. It was hard to imagine that any one of his Creoles had tried to wreck his boat, and was accepting Brandon's dirty money to do it. His men had worked hard this morning; they'd pulled on the cordelle line loyally.

"Any one of 'em on guard duty last night could o' done it," Jonas was saying. "Wouldn't even have to be somebody on guard duty. Any of 'em could o' gone on board an' put a sharp knife to that rope under the tarpaulin. Only take a second or two."

"Who was on guard duty last night?" Scot asked him.

Jonas went down the list. There had been nine men posted in three watches. When he came to the name Gaston Diderot, he stopped. Scot looked at him. Gaston was the little man who had permitted Nanette La Rue to go ashore. He hadn't liked the looks of Gaston, one of the last men they had signed aboard the Osage, but then crewmen had been hard to get back in St. Louis.

"What about Gaston?" Scot asked.

Jonas shrugged. "Said he'd been upriver before with

other outfits. Reckon that's all we know about him. St. Louis is full o' men like him. Maybe they'll put in a good day's work, an' maybe they'll stick a knife in your back to git it easier. You never kin tell."

Lucien Weatherby joined them. He, too, looked at the rope and then shook his head grimly. "The three of us who were aboard are lucky to be alive," he said, "and the loss of your boat would have stopped us from reaching the Blackfoot country this summer.

Scot said to Jonas, "Bring Gaston up here."

Jonas came back in a few moments, the little Creole trailing behind him, wiping his lips with the back of his hand. He'd just had his go at the brandy jug Scot had broken out as a reward for their valiant efforts.

Gaston was one of the smallest crew members, short, bowlegged, thick-shouldered, with a pointed chin and a black mustache. He looked at them curiously as he came up, and Scot pointed to the two ends of frayed rope on the ground.

"Take you long to cut through it, Gaston?" he asked.

The Creole looked at him stupidly, licking his lips with his tongue. His brown eyes were the eyes of a dog, quizzical, knowing that something was wrong, but not comprehending what it was.

"Out with it," Jonas Keene rasped. He slipped a knife from his belt and pushed the point against Gaston's stomach. "You cut that damned rope halfway through to wreck this boat, an' Cass Brandon paid you to do it. Ain't that right?"

"*Non!*" Gaston almost screeched, backing away a step.

85

He shook his head vigorously, looking down at the knife and then at the cordelle line.

"Brandon paid you off," Jonas grated. "You cut through that rope while you was on guard last flight."

Gaston was shaking his head, looking at Scot pleadingly. "Not me," he mumbled. "*Non.*"

"Put the knife away," Scot said. "Go on back to the crew, Gaston."

When the Creole had hurried off, Jonas Keene said, "Maybe if I'd started to carve on him a little, he'd o' opened up."

Scot shook his head. "I don't know," he said, and he looked at Lucien Weatherby.

The artist too had his doubts. "These French are great actors," he said, "but Gaston seemed honestly bewildered. It's hard to say."

"So now we know nothin'." Jonas scowled.

"We'll keep an eye on Gaston," Scot told him. "Watch him every step."

"The first move he makes," Jonas said, "he'll git that knife in his belly. I'm tellin' him that, too."

They went back to the Osage, and two of the crewmen coiled the long rope, stowing it again under the tarpaulin. They found Baptiste Privot up on his feet, feeling somewhat better after the brandy.

He grinned at Scot. "This is one tough river, *mon compagnon.*"

"The Missouri never whipped a good *voyageur.*"

"She come very close that time," Baptiste chuckled. "Sometime I think I am bes' man, an' then sometime I think of devil river is bes' man. Someday we shall see."

The river was deep again above the *embarras*. The oars were set up and the crewmen pulled away from the shore, Baptiste leading them in song. Scot, up on the cargo-box at the sweep, looked at Gaston pulling on one of the oars, and he wondered. He studied the other men, one by one. Most of them he knew well, men who had been with him before, and he knew he could trust them, but there were a half dozen who were new to him, the river scum like Gaston Diderot, who would risk their lives for the bourgeois, and then steal the pennies from his eyes when he was dead. The Creoles were unpredictable, as capricious as the river upon which they lived and died.

For the remainder of the morning they made good time with the oars, and then during the early afternoon hours a westerly breeze enabled them to set up the sail, and the men rested as the sail billowed out.

Lucien Weatherby was at the tiller sweep again, and Scot sat on the cargo-box with Jonas Keene, watching the river, noticing the way the big hills opened up to the west and north, leveling off, giving way to the vast rolling plains.

"Gittin' in to buffalo country now," Jonas said, "an' Injun country, too. Be hittin' the first Ree village tomorrow, an' then Sioux. Never had much use fer the Sioux, an' the Sioux don't have much use fer me."

"You think Brandon got by the *embarras?*" Scot asked him.

"Devil's allus with his kind," Jonas said. "He's comin' after us, but he ain't catchin' us. This crew kin row like hell, Scot, an' we got a faster boat than Brandon's."

"We'll have to stay ahead," Scot said soberly.

"Them Sioux are cute, too," Jonas went on musingly. "Play all kind o' tricks to git a keelboat in to the shore. Remember that big bay stallion they had tied in the meadow up at Crow Bend?"

Scot remembered the incident well. Two years before, as they had been ascending this same river in the keelboat St. Louis Belle, they had pulled in toward the shore, seeing a beautiful bay horse grazing in a meadow just off the river. The animal was not an Indian pony; it was much bigger and more powerfully proportioned.

Curious, they had poled in toward the shore, and within thirty yards of the bank Jonas Keene had spotted the halter trailing through the high grass in the meadow. They had backed away hastily just as a swarm of Sioux arrows came from the willows along the bank, and they had realized then that the horse in the meadow had been a ruse to draw them in toward the shore. Two crewmen had died because they had been curious, and although the Sioux had tried again on different occasions to entice them in toward the shore with burning campfires and other devices, Scot had never again gone for the bait.

Now, once again, they were entering Sioux country, and undoubtedly the wily Sioux already knew of their presence, and were watching them from behind those barren brown hills.

"Nothin' the Sioux like better than to burn a river boat," Jonas Keene was saying, "an' to take trappers' hair."

Scot packed his pipe and puffed on it thoughtfully. He watched Nanette La Rue come out of the cabin, dressed

88

in the bright red and white blouse she had claimed to have thrown into the river. She came up onto the roof of the cargo-box and sat down next to Scot, smiling at him.

Jonas Keene said, "Them Sioux ain't seen us yet, they will now with that skirt, Nanette."

"You do not like?" Nanette laughed.

"I like," the trapper growled. "Sioux like, too."

"You like?" Nanette said to Scot, arching her dark head, her dark eyes softening.

Scot took the pipe from his mouth. "Along this part of the river," he said, "it would be better for you to wear the boy's clothes."

"Very well," Nanette said. "You like me, Monsieur Scot?"

Scot felt himself reddening. "Better get inside." He scowled. "The Sioux might like you, too, and that wouldn't be good."

Nanette laughed merrily and jumped down from the box. As she was ducking in through the low door of the little cabin, Jonas Keene said, "She's a woman, Scot."

Scot took the pipe from his mouth and looked at it. He knew it; he knew it too well.

## Chapter Eight

For eight days they pushed steadily north and west up the big river, moving through the low hills, seeing the giant buffalo herds, sometimes on both sides of the river, stretching from horizon to horizon, blackening the landscape.

They stopped at a friendly Ree village, and Scot had a

talk with the chief, Blue Feather, as the Creoles cruised through the town seeking likely squaws.

Nanette La Rue remained on board, and when Scot came back alone to the keelboat she was pouting. "You like these Indian girls?"

Scot shrugged. "Ree women are supposed to be the best lookers on the Missouri," he said. "A good many trappers prefer them to the women of New Orleans and St. Louis."

Nanette looked at him blackly. "I do not like you," she said.

Scot grinned, blue eyes twinkling. "Only squaw I saw in the village was Blue Feather's wife. She's near seventy."

He sat on the edge of the cargo-box, watching Lucien Weatherby sketching a young Ree in full war dress. Weatherby had given the Indian an ax and enticed him aboard to have his picture drawn. A dozen other Rees had sought to come aboard to watch, but Jonas Keene had shooed them off.

"Friendly Indians." Scot had smiled at him.

"Country's full o' dead men," Jonas told him, "killed by friendly Indians. We ain't takin' no chances."

Nanette took her seat next to Scot. She said, "You have an Indian girl up at Fort Adams."

Scot frowned. "Carole is part Cheyenne," he admitted. "I never said she was my girl."

"I will be your girl."

Scot bit his lips. "All right," he said impatiently. "All right."

Weatherby said to him from his easel, "What does

Blue Feather have to say, Scot?"

"He claims the Sioux are getting tougher all the time. They're trying to push the Rees out of this country."

Weatherby nodded. "I know many Sioux," he said. "Some of the Ogalalas are all right. The Brulés are bad. They'll kill you first and ask your business later."

"Plenty of Sioux upriver," Scot said. "Blue Feather's men have had a run-in with them. That means we'll see them, too."

"Keep that cannon loaded and ready," Weatherby advised. "They don't like cannon. It's the noise gets them. Jonas is probably more effective with his rifle than the cannon, but they're afraid of the cannon."

Scot nodded. He watched the artist cleverly sketching the Indian with his pencils, the young Indian standing there proudly, gripping his bow, an eagle feather trailing from his crow-black hair, black eyes glittering.

Jonas Keene had gone upriver with a few Indian pack horses to shoot buffalo. He came trailing back now, the two horses loaded down with fresh meat, and Scot welcomed him aboard.

"Plenty Injun sign," Jonas grunted. "Bad Injuns."

Romaine, the cook, got a fire going in the sand box on board and roasted a few of the buffalo steaks, but even this could not entice the Creoles back aboard. Scot could hear Baptiste Privot's booming laugh from the village as darkness came, and then the squeals of the Ree women.

Romaine stepped ashore, eating hastily. Lucien Weatherby finished his sketch in the firelight, and then went to the village to visit with Blue Feather. Jonas Keene, always restless, went prowling ashore with his rifle, moving upriver, cruising downriver to see if he could spot Cass Brandon's firelight.

Scot smoked his pipe aboard alone, and then Nanette La Rue came out of the cabin as he leaned against the mast, watching the firelight flicker on Indian tepees ashore. He saw Baptiste stride through the village, a Ree girl on either arm, his bright red woolen cap pushed back on his head, white teeth flashing as he laughed.

Nanette said thoughtfully, "You are a trapper, and you do not go ashore like the other men."

Scot just shrugged. "Figured I'd keep an eye on the boat tonight. Crew are entitled to a rest."

"I am so glad you find me in St. Louis."

"You found us." Scot smiled, remembering that she'd been a stowaway. "How did you know the Osage was our boat?"

"I ask." Nanette grinned. "I find out, and I follow you that night after the fight."

"You were pretty anxious to come with us."

"You know why?"

Scot looked down at her. He could see her face dimly in the light of the lantern on the cargo-box roof. She was standing in front of him, looking up at him.

"I know why," he said. Then he reached forward and pulled her roughly toward him and kissed her full on the mouth, and even as he did so he was thinking of Carole Du Bois, who had asked him to hurry north.

"You are good man," Nanette whispered. "You do not go ashore like others."

"I don't have to go ashore," Scot murmured. He would have kissed her again, but this time he didn't, and he wasn't sure why. Even though he had thought much of Carole this winter back in St. Louis, he was not engaged to her. Between them there had been only friendship. Possibly she had already met someone upriver, a trader or trapper, but Scot knew this was unlikely.

Nanette La Rue was looking up at him quizzically. "You do not like me?"

Scot released her, knowing that it was over. He did like Nanette. She was a bewitching girl, but he had to know about Carole first. He had to settle it in his mind about Carole, because if he didn't he would be miserable until he saw her upriver.

"Reckon I'd better go ashore," Scot said.

"You are a fool," Nanette said simply. "You are one bigger fool than even you think you are."

Crossing the plank to the shore, Scot thought about that. He stopped and turned around, looking back at her. She was still standing by the mast, the lantern light falling full across her face. There was a peculiar expression on her face. She was angry with him, but that was not all. She was saddened, also, and this he did not understand. A girl like Nanette La Rue was not often sad.

"*Bon soir,*" Nanette said.

"Good night," Scot answered. He stepped ashore and went again to see Blue Feather, and found him chatting amiably with Lucien Weatherby, who spoke the Ree tongue as well as Scot himself. It was late when they returned to the Osage, to find Jonas Keene back and establishing the guard for the night.

The Creoles returned to the shore encampment one by one, Baptiste Privot coming in last, a tall, light-skinned Ree girl with him. Baptiste looked at Scot, raising his eyebrows slightly, grinning in amusement.

"*Non?*" he asked.

"No." Scot shook his head. "Send her back, Baptiste." Baptiste shooed the girl back to the village, and then rolled in his blanket near the shore fire.

Jonas came over and sat down next to Scot near the fire. He said, "A new start in the mornin'."

Scot nodded.

"An' we'll keep that damn cannon loaded an' ready fer bear—or Sioux."

Again Scot nodded. He watched the crack of light around the cabin on board the Osage, and he wondered if he'd made a mistake this night. Only time would tell.

They left the Ree village at dawn with wood smoke curling up from half a hundred tepees along the bank and a crowd of the curious down at the water's edge to see them go.

The aged Blue Feather stood on the bank, making strange motions with his hands, and Scot said to Jonas Keene, "What is he saying?"

"Watch the Sioux."

"We're not forgetting them." Scot smiled faintly.

They made good time that morning with a westerly breeze blowing and the sail up. Early in the afternoon the wind stopped and they broke out the oars. Jonas Keene went ashore in the morning, cut overland as the Osage swung around several elbow bends, and came ashore at noon, shaking his head at Scot.

"Any sign?" Scot asked him.

"None of 'em around," Jonas growled, "an' that's what I'm worried about. When you don't see 'em, watch out."

"We'll stay out in mid-river," Scot said, "until we camp tonight, and we'll see if we can find an island on which to camp."

He noticed that the crewmen were silent now, eying the banks as they rowed; all except big Baptiste, who stood up in the bow with his pole, singing as usual, undaunted.

Scot was at the handle of the sweep when they swung around a wide bend of the river, the Creoles pulling lustily, and then he nearly fell from the roof of the cargo-box. He straightened up, staring, and he saw Jonas Keene rising slowly to his feet in front of him.

There was a small promontory just around the big bend of the river, an outcropping of rock rising ten feet above the water's edge, and standing on the rock, looking straight at them as they slipped around the bend, was Carole Du Bois.

At a distance of less than fifty yards Scot recognized her immediately. She stood on the rock, tall and straight, her black hair drawn back in braids. She wore a skirt of dressed fawnskin, and a green velvet jacket he had seen her wearing many times up at the trading post. Jonas looked back at Scot. He said softly, "Carole."

She saw them. She saw Scot up on the cargo-box, and she was looking straight at him, but she made no sign to him. Her hands hung loose at her sides.

Baptiste Privot had seen her also, and he turned to look back at Scot and point. Some of the crew stopped rowing to turn and look.

Instinctively Scot swung the Osage in toward the promontory, a thousand thoughts running through his mind. Carole had come downriver looking for help for her father, or the trading post had been raided by hostile Sioux, and she'd had to flee, but she was alone on the rock promontory, and there was no sign of joy on her face as they drew near her. She did not call out or wave to them.

Jonas Keene said softly, "Somethin' damn funny here, Scot."

"Carole," Scot called. "Carole."

Nanette La Rue came out of the cabin, hearing him shout, and she too stared at the half-breed girl standing so silently on the rock.

They were within thirty yards of the promontory, still edging in, when Carole Du Bois came to life. She gestured with her right hand, waving them back, at the same time calling sharply, "No! No, Scot! Sioux!"

"Ambush," Jonas Keene grated, and he leaped toward the brass cannon in the bow.

At the same time Carole Du Bois dived gracefully toward the water, a flight of arrows coming after her from the willows and the rocks along the shoreline. The fierce Sioux war cry broke out from behind a rock barricade, and then a tall Indian raced up to the small cliff from which Carole had dived. She hit the water cleanly, came to the surface with her black hair glistening, and swam for the Osage, taking long, clean strokes.

The Indian on the wall drew back his how and an arrow whistled through the air, lifting a small gusher of water from a point inches to Carole's left. More arrows were coming from the shore. One of them shivered into the mast. Scot heard several more whisper past him. A Creole at the oars gasped as a feathered shaft sank into his shoulder.

The Sioux on the cliff was fitting another arrow to his bow when Lucien Weatherby, who had been sprawled on the cargo-box, snatched up a rifle, raised it swiftly, and fired.

The Indian with the bow pitched forward off the cliff, hitting the water with a splash. At the same time the Osage's cannon boomed, Jonas Keene having reached it with his lighted pipe.

The four-pound shot crashed through the trees beyond the rocks, immediately silencing the Sioux shouts. The Creoles at the oars had ducked down when the flight of arrows came, and the Osage was beginning to drift back, away from the promontory, away from Carole Du Bois, who was swimming hard to reach them.

"The oars!" Scot shouted. "Pick up the oars!"

He could see the brown shapes sliding among the rocks and willows along the shore. "A few of the more venturesome of the Sioux sent arrows at them, but the majority had fallen back, frightened by that roar from the small cannon.

Lucien Weatherby was down on the catwalk, a coil of rope in his hand. As the Creoles bent to the oars again at Scot's order and the Osage moved slowly forward, Weatherby tossed the rope toward the swimming girl.

Jonas Keene had the four-pounder ready again, and another shot whipped toward the shore. He aimed lower this time, and the ball tore through the willows, bouncing like a mad thing through the rocks beyond. The caroming shot caught a Sioux on the run, knocking him off his feet, sending him rolling, screaming.

Carole caught the rope and Weatherby pulled her toward the boat and helped her aboard as the Osage moved past the promontory, Scot guiding the boat out into mid-river.

Carole came up along the catwalk, river water streaming from her. She looked up at Scot, and this time she smiled. Nanette was staring at her curiously.

Scot said to the French girl, "Take her into the cabin. Give her your skirt and blouse until her own clothes dry."

"How are you, Scot?" Carole said in perfect English.

She was taller than Nanette, and her hair was raven black, with a sheen to it. Her features were small and even, her eyes brown. When she smiled at Scot she revealed small white teeth. She spoke in a low, musical voice. Her cheekbones were slightly higher than a white girl's.

"Are you all right, Carole?" Scot asked her. "The Sioux didn't hurt you?"

"I'm all right."

When she had gone into the cabin, Jonas Keene came up on the cargo-box. They had left the promontory behind with its yelling, disappointed Sioux. Jonas said, "They used Carole this time instead o' that bay horse."

Scot nodded grimly.

"She hadn't warned us off," Jonas added, "we'd o' been dead men by now. Must o' been two hundred of 'em along that shore. What do you figure she's doin' down this way, Scot?"

Scot just shook his head. "The Sioux captured her," he said. "They were using her to take our boat."

"Must be bad news up at Adams, then," Jonas murmured.

"It can't be good," Scot agreed.

Lucien Weatherby joined them on the cargo-box. He said, "Another close one, Scot. That girl has nerve."

"They had an arrow on her back every moment that she stood there," Jonas agreed. "That jump into the river fooled 'em, though."

"She could always swim like a fish." Scot smiled. "Guess the Sioux didn't know that."

In a few minutes Carole came out of the cabin dressed in Nanette's bright red skirt and the white blouse, and she was no longer an Indian girl. Her hair was pulled into a bun at the back. Her skin seemed even lighter in color. She climbed lithely up to the cargo-box, Nanette watching her with reluctant admiration. She gave Scot her hand as she came up, a warm, firm hand, and she said, "I'm sorry if I nearly caused you to lose your boat, Scot. They forced me to stand out on the rocks."

"I know," Scot said.

Lucien Weatherby bowed pleasantly to Carole, and she smiled back at him. Weatherby said, "I'll take the tiller if you want to talk, Scot. You must have a lot to say."

Gratefully Scot stepped away from the sweep handle.

He moved up to the bow with Carole, noticing how much more mature she was now than she had been last summer. In one year she had become a beautiful woman. He said, "I didn't bring you toys this time, Carole." They sat down on the edge of the cargo-box, and he looked at her steadily. He said, "The Sioux captured you? Tell me about it."

Carole's dark eyes clouded. "Father died several months ago, a week after I sent the letter to you. There was trouble at the post after that. I—I had to leave."

"They molested you?" Scot growled. "Who was it?"

Carole shook her head. "It will do no good to punish anyone, Scot. There was a band of Gros Ventres at the post, and some Crows. Then the half-breed clerks began to pay too much attention to me. I knew I had to leave."

"You went alone?" Scot asked her incredulously.

"I thought I could reach Fort Tecumseh."

"Tecumseh is above here," Scot reminded her.

Carole nodded. "I never reached the Army post," she explained. "The Sioux caught me above Tecumseh. I was coming downriver in a canoe. I had plenty of supplies, and I traveled only at night. They caught me in my camp one morning."

"How long ago?"

"Four days," Carole told him. "They knew a keelboat was coming upriver, and they thought they could use me to help them take it."

"They almost succeeded," Scot growled. "So they took you down around Tecumseh. Was it bad?"

Carole smiled a little. "Don't forget I'm part Indian," she said. "I knew how to handle them. I told them I wouldn't help them catch you if they harmed me."

"You're brave," Scot said. "I'm sorry about your father. Jacques was a good friend. Empire Fur Company will miss him." He paused and then he said, "What about the post? Are the clerks still running it?"

Carole shook her head. "There had been a lot of drinking before I left, and that's why I was able to get away without being seen. I'm afraid you won't find much of the post left."

"We'll see when we get there," Scot grated. "Those boys will pay for any damage they've done.

"I'm afraid they'll be gone," Carole told him. "You're setting up another post above Adams?"

Scot nodded. "We came upriver for that reason," he explained. "We're going into the Blackfoot country."

Carole grimaced. Then she glanced back over her shoulder. "I didn't think you would have a woman aboard, Scot. Is she your wife?"

"Stowaway," Scot said, reddening a little. "I had intended to leave her with you at Adams so she could help take care of your father. Now she'll have to stay at Tecumseh."

"I, too?" Carole asked slowly.

Scot rubbed his jaw. "We'll see," he said. He was remembering that Carole was part Indian, and an Indian girl at an Army barracks, particularly a tiny one like Fort Tecumseh, might not be too safe. Nanette could take care of herself, and the officers of the post would see she wasn't harmed, but they might not be too concerned about a breed girl, a beautiful one like Carole Du Bois. She would be looked upon as fair game.

101

"I would like to go with you to the Blackfoot country," Carole was saying. "My father would have wanted that, Scot."

"I know." Scot nodded. A girl like Carole, who had just traveled alone several hundred miles down the wildest part of the Missouri, would not be in the way. She could take care of herself in the wilderness.

"This other girl won't like it if you take me," Carole said, "and leave her behind. Isn't that right?"

Scot grimaced. "Miss La Rue is not a passenger on this boat," he stated. "We wanted to put her off at Leavenworth."

"And she would not go."

"We had trouble," Scot admitted.

"She won't go to Tecumseh, either," Carole said simply. "You don't know women, Scot."

Scot knew that she was right. They were going to have more trouble with Nanette at Tecumseh, which they would reach in two or three days. He wished now that he had been a little more adamant back at Leavenworth, but at that time Nanette's own solution had seemed the best, and he still didn't like to cast the French girl adrift. She was alone in the world; she needed help, and she did like him. He wondered if the fact that she was a white girl while Carole was part Indian had anything to do with it. He'd seen what had happened to other trappers and traders when they settled down with Indian women. Never did the Indian change; it was always the white man who took on the red man's indolence and sloth. Gradually the drive left him, and he sat in his cabin door, smoking his pipe, wondering what had happened to him, no better than the savage sitting out in front of his tepee, puffing on his clay pipe, content to watch the sun rise and go down, to eat and to drink, and to see his children grow up, and when he died there was nothing left to mark where he'd been or what he'd been.

He didn't want that, but looking at Carole, he was a little ashamed of these thoughts. Carole had spent a few years in Quebec with her father. She had French blood in her, and the best French blood. Jacques Du Bois's ancestry had been of the aristocracy. She had a better education than most white girls on the frontier, but still she'd had a Cheyenne mother, and Scot MacGregor had still to find out how much influence that dead Cheyenne woman would have upon her daughter. He'd seen the influence it had had upon Jacques Du Bois himself. Jacques could have been a bourgeois. With his many talents and his background he could have set up his own fur company, dispatching his traders and trappers up the various forks of the Missouri and the Yellowstone. Instead, he'd settled down at a tiny trading post with a Cheyenne woman, and the mountain fever had eventually done for him.

Looking over his shoulder, Scot saw Nanette watching them from the other end of the cargo-box. She was a beautiful girl, and he had to admit that she'd brightened this trip up a lonely river. A man would be a fool to cast her aside lightly, especially when she had already intimated that she liked him.

"You don't know women, Scot," Carole Du Bois had said.

Scot MacGregor did not question that statement.

# Chapter Nine

They reached Fort Tecumseh at high noon three days after picking up Carole Du Bois. As the Creoles rowed in toward the landing place, singing happily, Scot waited for the boom of Tecumseh's welcoming cannon.

It did not come. The log ramparts stood on a hillock fifty yards up from the river, two corner bastions commanding all approaches to the ten-foot walls. The brass six-pounder stood in the little gatehouse over the entrance way. The flag fluttered from the mast above the gatehouse, but there was no cannon shot.

Scot stood up in the bow of the Osage with Jonas Keene, staring at the shore. A log raft was drawn up at the little wharf and a pirogue was pulled up on the shore, but the wharf was empty.

"What do you make of it, Jonas?" Scot asked. He glanced back at Weatherby, who was at the tiller, and Weatherby shook his head in perplexity.

"Ain't no doubt somebody seen us comin' up," Jonas muttered. "We been in sight on this river fer ten minutes now. Where in hell is everybody?"

They were within fifty yards of the dock now, moving in slowly. Scot lifted his voice and shouted, "Fort Tecumseh! Fort Tecumseh!"

There was no return hail, no heads lifting up above the log ramparts from the firing platforms.

"That gate," Jonas Keene murmured, "is open. I don't like it, Scot."

"There were seventy-five men stationed at Tecumseh

last fall. Your friend Haggerty passed through here less than two months ago."

"That's right," Jonas said, "but there ain't nobody hailin' us, an' seventy-five men can't all be deaf at the same time."

"Captain Lorimer may have taken his men out against the Sioux," Scot suggested.

"An' left the fort unguarded? Not a man left?"

Lifting his rifle, Jonas fired it into the air when they were twenty yards from the dock. A flock of buzzards lifted up into the air from inside the fort as the echoes of the rifle shot reverberated upriver.

Scot heard Jonas Keene catch his breath and then say slowly, "Carrion. Reckon this is bad, Scot."

"You think they've been wiped out?"

"No one livin' in that post," Jonas said. "No Injuns around, either. Them birds would have been sittin' up on the walls or in trees if anybody was around."

Carole Du Bois came up to the bow to join Scot. She said, "I don't understand this."

"Them Sioux that captured you," Jonas asked her, "say anything about raidin' Fort Tecumseh?"

Carole shook her head. "They would have had fresh scalps. There were no scalps with that band."

"The post is empty," Scot told her.

Carole nodded. "I saw the birds," she murmured.

The Osage slid up alongside the wharf, Baptiste poling carefully, and Scot stepped ashore. He went up the pathway to the fort gate at a fast walk, Jonas following him. Inside they could hear the buzzards quarreling, and as they approached the gate a coyote slunk out through the opening, dashing away through the bushes.

The main gate swung listlessly on its hinges. Scot pushed it aside and stepped in. He stopped just inside the gate, looking around. There were no arrows stuck in the walls of the fort, but a slaughter had taken place inside. The stripped, scalped bodies of the soldiers were scattered around the little parade ground in front of the headquarters building. They lay there like rag dolls carelessly tossed aside by a child. There was no shape and no form to them. Some men lay on their backs, sightless eyes staring up at the blue sky; others lay on their stomachs or huddled on their sides. Two men were sprawled on the firing platform near the gate, but they had been shot from the inside of the post.

"Surprised 'em," Jonas muttered. "Looks like the whole damn post is wiped out, Scot. They got in here some way, an' it was all over in a matter o' minutes. Our boys never had a chance."

"When?" Scot asked dully.

"Yesterday," Jonas said. "Two days ago. No more than that. It was after we picked up Carole. Could o' been the same crowd, an' a bunch o' others joined up with 'em."

"You know how they got in?"

Jonas shrugged. "Them Sioux are clever," he said, "an' these poor boys weren't lookin' fer trouble. They could o' floated downriver on that old Army log raft, an' then bust in here when the gate was open. Some of 'em could o' come down on the raft, an' the others waited back in the hills. Once they were inside it didn't last long."

Carole Du Bois was trailing up from the boat, and when Scot saw her he waved her back. Lucien Weatherby and Baptiste Privot came up to the gate and looked inside. Weatherby said to Jonas, "You think any of them are still around, Jonas?"

The lean hunter shook his head. "Injuns are funny," he said. "They win a big fight like this an' they have to go back an' tell somebody about it. The bunch that smashed up this place are headin' back fer their village so's they kin talk about their victory."

"Call up the crew," Scot told Baptiste. "Bring shovels. All we can do for these poor fellows is to bury them."

Walking back to the Osage, Jonas said to Scot, "Reckon you'll have to change your plans again, Scot."

"How's that?" Scot asked him.

"You ain't leavin' Nanette La Rue here," Jonas said, "an' there ain't no place above here where she kin stay, either. She goes with us, or you turn around an' head back fer Leavenworth—eight hundred miles."

Scot looked at him and shook his head.

"Two women aboard," Jonas murmured, "an' we're headin' up into Blackfoot country."

"And Brandon's still behind us," Scot growled. "If we lose one day he goes ahead of us, and we're in for real trouble."

"You ain't forgettin', either," Jonas added, "that we got somebody aboard the Osage who's workin' fer Brandon."

"You been watching Gaston?" Scot asked him.

"Watchin' him," Jonas said, "but if it's him, he's bein' smart. Just layin' low an' doin' nothin'."

Baptiste Privot led the Creoles up the hill to bury the dead inside the fort walls. Nanette La Rue watched from the deck of the Osage. When Scot came aboard she said, "All the poor soldiers have been killed?"

"That's right," Scot said. "Massacre."

"It is terrible."

"This is rough country," Scot agreed.

Nanette was looking at him steadily. "I will have to go with you," she said. "There is no Fort Tecumseh, and no Fort Adams."

Scot looked across the river. "That's right."

"Then I am glad," Nanette smiled, "even though you like this other girl."

"I wish you hadn't come," Scot told her, "for your own sake. It's going to be a tough trip and a hard winter upriver."

"I am glad to go," Nanette said. "I am not afraid."

Scot said no more on the subject. It took several hours for the crew to dig shallow graves for the dead soldiers, and it was nearly dusk when they went aboard the Osage and rowed north a few miles to camp on an island in mid-river.

It was a silent, gloomy encampment, the terrible massacre at Fort Tecumseh having put everyone in low spirits. The Creoles did not laugh and sing tonight. After eating they wrapped themselves in their blankets and stared at the fire, or looked apprehensively across the river toward the far shore.

There was no moon tonight, but the stars were big and bright, speckling the sky. Upriver, a hawk sounded, and then a screech owl whisked by in the brush on the island,

and the Creoles around the campfire hunched deeper in their blankets.

Scot watched Jonas Keene get up without a word, shake the ash out of his pipe, and put the pipe into his pocket. Then Jonas stepped into the quarter boat and pushed out from the shore without speaking to anyone. He disappeared in the darkness, headed for the west bank of the river, and they could hear the faint swish of his oars as he propelled the small boat, and then that was gone too.

Seated by the fire, watching Lucien Weatherby working again on one of his sketches in the firelight, Scot thought of Jonas—always restless in Indian country, always watching, traveling in the daytime, prowling at night, listening, looking, smelling for danger.

That was the way it had been up in the Blackfoot country when they'd trapped through those cold winters, the knowledge with them every moment that one slip, one sign missed, and they were dead. It was a hard way to make a living, but Scot had never known a mountain man who would exchange it for another way. The big mountains got inside of you, and you could never get them out—mountains and meadows and cold, clear streams, and the beaver slipping through the glassy calm water of their damned-up streams.

Carole Du Bois sat across the fire from him, sewing on her buckskin dress, every once in a while her dark eyes lifting to him, smiling a little, but saying nothing, and that was the Indian in her. She would talk with him when he wanted to talk, and she would be silent when he had his own thoughts. A white woman was not like that.

Nanette La Rue had been at the campfire too, but she had gone aboard to the cabin. Carole also slept on board, but under a tarpaulin lean-to in the bow.

Lucien Weatherby said, nodding after Jonas Keene, "What will he do when the land fills up? He owns the mountains now, but it won't always be that way."

"He'll go deeper into the hills," Scot said and half-smiled, "like a wounded bull moose. He won't live long enough to see it crowded."

Weatherby shook his head. "Coming quicker than you think, Scot," he said. "I've been east. I've heard the talk. Men want land, cheap land, and all the good land is taken back east. In ten years you'll see the wagons coming through this way as thick as the mosquitoes around us now."

"It's a good country on the other side of the mountains," Scot agreed.

"You'll go there someday yourself?" Weatherby asked, glancing up at him from the sketch.

Scot shrugged. "Hard to say."

"You're not made like Jonas Keene," Weatherby told him. "The fur animals won't last forever. When they're gone you'll have to start over again, Scot. You don't want to hole up in the deep hills. They'll be needing men like you down along the Columbia in the Oregon Territory. They'll need leaders who know the land."

Carole Du Bois was listening as she sewed, and Scot saw her nod her head very slightly in agreement.

"Big job now," he said, "is to open the way with these

110

posts, and make it American soil."

He looked out across the dark water, and then over at the Osage, rocking very gently with the moving river. There was a crack of light around Nanette La Rue's door. He was thinking that it wasn't only the Blackfeet that could stop him from carrying out his dream, and it wasn't only Brandon; a woman could stop him marrying the wrong woman, a woman who was not for him.

At breakfast the next morning Jonas Keene drank his black coffee and then said to Scot, "Brandon camped three miles below Fort Tecumseh last night. Saw his fire."

"Right on our heels," Scot said. "One slip and he's past us."

"Won't be our slip," Jonas told him.

They used the poles that morning, working steadily up a river that narrowed each day, and each day became more wild. It was a big country, a sprawling country of open plains and rolling hills, and beyond were the big mountains with the snow gleaming on their summits, and each day they drew nearer to those mountains.

The Missouri boiled down at them, brown and turgid with its cargo of dead, stinking buffalo and drifting trees. Here and there along the banks they saw Indian scaffolds, holding the dead, with the buzzards perched on them. They passed Sioux encampments along the river, long abandoned encampments with a few old tepee poles still standing, the land bare and trodden down with the grass just beginning to grow again.

The tortuous curves of the Missouri were more pronounced as they ascended the river, and one day they poled for ten hours to make three miles on a river that bent and twisted like a snake on the ground.

Again they were held up for half a day as a great herd of buffalo swam the river in front of them, the huge, ungainly animals caving in the sandbanks as they lumbered down into the water, filling it with their humped backs, an unending stream of them.

Jonas Keene shot buffalo and elk and mule-tailed deer, bringing in the choice parts. Meat was plentiful along here, and would be all the way to the mountains.

They saw no Indians. Occasional streamers of smoke lifted into the air from the distant hills where Indian bands were encamped, but none of them came to the river, and for this Scot was grateful.

Already they were getting beyond the Sioux hunting grounds, but they were still far from the land of the Blackfeet. The Blackfeet villages were farther north and west in the higher mountains and the deep, vast meadows, prime trapping grounds for both red and white men.

At times the gnats and mosquitoes made life almost unbearable for them along the river, and Scot had smoke fires built in the sand box on the keelboat where Nanette La Rue and Carole could sit, their heads in the smoke, the only protection against the fierce insects.

There was no relief, though, for the Creoles at the poles or along the shore with the cordelle line, stumbling through the marshes, sloshing through mud and brush, raising clouds of mosquitoes around their heads. They cursed and slapped and pulled on the line with one hand,

and they cursed more, and at night their faces were puffed out of shape by the bites, and they had to plaster their faces with river mud to bring relief.

They passed the mouth of the Yellowstone, a big river surging into the Missouri, adding its own quota of silt and dead trees and dead buffalo. A thousand streams and creeks flowed into the Missouri, into the larger rivers like the Yellowstone and the Powder and the Little Missouri and the Cheyenne, all of them adding water and sand and silt to the big tide flowing ever out of the north and west.

Daily Scot stood at the tiller handle, steering around the drifting trees as the men rowed or poled, or as the wind carried them onward. He set Jonas Keene ashore on one point, picking him up hours later at another when he saw the hunter standing silently on a promontory, sometimes flashing a bit of mirror to attract his attention.

Always Jonas reported that Brandon was still coming, a day, a half day's journey behind them, both crews hardened to the river now, toiling in the hot sun, their clothes in rags, bodies browned, blackened. They stumbled through the brush along the banks pulling the cordelle line, and from a distance they looked like a pack of savage wolves.

Nearing the mountains they ran into foul weather. A rain squall hit them in the late afternoon as they were poling slowly up along the west bank of the river. The black clouds had been building up all during the morning, and the storm struck in the afternoon. Scot had been hoping to make an island at the mouth of Sand Creek, but the storm hit them when they were still a mile or so below the island. It struck with unbridled fury, the rain lashing at them, the wind driving downriver.

Scot had been turning the Osage in toward the east bank and a sheltered cove there, but the storm hit them so suddenly that the keelboat was swung around in the river, and several of the Creoles were nearly blown off the catwalk.

Baptiste Privot worked his pole furiously, and with the wind tearing at them, driving them downriver, Scot managed to swing the Osage in toward the bank.

Jonas Keene went over the side with a rope, swimming through the rain-pocked water, almost lost in the sheets of rain whirling over him. Scot sent two other men to the shore with additional ropes to lash the Osage securely to the bank, and then he ordered Carole into the cabin with Nanette. Carole had been on deck when the storm broke, and she was as wet as if she had been in the river when she stepped into the cabin.

There was no shelter for the crew, and no time to throw up tarpaulins. The wind would have whipped them away before they could have been set up.

With the Osage snubbed to the bank, the Creoles crouched on the lee side of the cargo-box, protected to some extent from the driving rain. Scot sat with Jonas Keene and Lucien Weatherby, holding a tarpaulin over their heads, their backs against the cargo-box. The rain splattered down against the tarpaulin. They could hear the wind driving through the tall cottonwood trees along the bank, bending them, cracking off smaller branches, and Jonas turned to shout in Scot's ear, "Too close to them trees."

Scot had seen that, too, but there was nothing they could do about it. He realized, then, that he'd made his mistake in not pulling in toward the shore an hour or so ago and seeking a sheltered cove where there were not too many tall trees that could come crashing down across the boat.

Lucien Weatherby said consolingly, "It might blow over quickly."

They could feel the Osage rising and falling beneath them. Rain trickled in under the tarpaulin, running down their necks. Scot looked out to see how the crewmen were doing, and saw that they had also dragged a tarpaulin over them and were huddled under it, waiting for the storm to pass.

As he looked he saw the tops of the tallest trees, some of them forty feet high, swaying perilously. The wind seemed to be increasing in velocity. Farther back in the fringe of timber along the river trees were cracking, going down under the strain, and then a tall cottonwood along the bank started to sway, reaching out over the bow of the Osage. There was a crack like the report of a pistol and the tree fell, crashing down across the bow of the keelboat, just missing the cargo-box.

The mast went down, ripped off by overhanging branches and heavy limbs. There was the splintering sound of wood giving way beneath the strain. The bow of the Osage went down and the keel came up out of the water. Scot felt himself being rammed back against the wall of the cargo-box as the keelboat tipped up. He heard the Creoles yelling in fear, and the sickening thought came to him that this was the end of the trip here along the bank of the Missouri, the end of all the planning and sweating and worrying, the slow and endless hours working their way up a stubborn and devilish river. It could be the end, too, of a dream of empire.

## *Chapter Ten*

The stern of the Osage lifted higher and higher until it was fully five feet out of the water with the bow pushed down to the water line by the weight of the stricken tree.

Scot scrambled from beneath the tarpaulin, working his way down the slippery, inclined deck to the cabin. He noticed that the crew had been tumbled down along the catwalk in the direction of the tree across the bow, and they were now picking themselves up dazedly. Several had been shaken into the river, and they were swimming back to the boat, clambering to the deck, the rain pelting down on them.

The cabin door opened when Scot came up to it and Carole Du Bois put her head out.

"Break out the axes," Scot told her. There were a dozen long-handled woodsmen's axes stacked in the cabin to be used when they built the trading post in the Blackfeet country. Carole started to hand them out, and Scot shoved them at Jonas Keene, Lucien Weatherby, and Baptiste Privot as they came up, knowing what they had to do without being told.

The four of them worked their way in among the branches of the huge tree, swinging the axes, lopping off limbs, pushing them into the river. Baptiste Privot moved out across the main trunk of the tree, which was

116

nearly two feet in diameter, and began to hack away like a madman, ax rising and falling rhythmically.

"Git the weight off her," Jonas Keene panted. "That water comes in over the bow an' we're licked."

They worked with the rain pelting down on them and the wind tugging at them as they scrambled among the tree limbs, cutting, pushing, lightening the weight on the bow so that the Osage would settle back into the water.

As he hacked away at a stubborn limb, Scot Mac-Gregor watched the water line. Some water had seeped in over the bow of the boat, but already with the tree limbs being chopped off the load was less than it had been, and the bow had come up—an inch, two inches.

In ten minutes the four of them swinging the axes had stripped the tree trunk clean, and Baptiste Privot was nearly through the main trunk of the tree. The weight of the big log was still upon them, however, and the Osage was tipped at a perilous angle.

When Baptiste had finally cut his way through the log, Scot called for more hands to help, and a dozen of them rolled the trunk off the bow into the water. The Osage immediately righted itself, quivering like a bruised animal.

The four of them with the axes sat down on the deck, oblivious of the rain now, letting it pelt down upon them. They sat there with the axes at their sides, panting, unable to speak, the rain trickling down their faces. Nanette La Rue and Carole looked out through the cabin door at them, and Carole shook her head in sympathy.

Jonas Keene said to Scot, "Never figured we'd do it, Scot. Must be eight or ten feet o' water along here.

Enough to cover this boat if she'd gone under."

Scot looked over at Baptiste Privot. Baptiste's big shoulders were heaving. Of the four, he had put in the biggest lick on the trunk of the tree. Standing on the slippery wood, he had swung his ax faster than Scot had ever seen one swung before, hacking huge chips out of the wood with each stroke.

Baptiste managed to grin, and he said, "Ol' devil river. She almos' catch Baptiste that time, *mon compagnon*."

Jonas went over to have a look at the lines holding the Osage to the bank. All of the lines had held firm. He came back to look at the mast, which had been broken off at the deck line, and he shook his head in disgust. It meant they would have to take time out on the morrow to cut down a straight pole and make a mast out of it.

"Letting up," Lucien Weatherby said to Scot, and he nodded toward the tops of the trees along the bank. The wind still tore through them, but they were not bending so much as before, and the rain seemed to be lessening too.

The Creoles had made a feeble attempt to draw the tarpaulin back around them, but most of them had given it up as a bad job, and were content to let the rain soak them through, knowing that they could dry out once they got a few fires going on the shore.

The squall was over in another half hour, and the sun made a weak effort to come out before dropping behind the western hills, leaving a truly magnificent sunset.

The plank was run ashore and the crew scrambled about for dry firewood. They had several large fires going in a few minutes and were warming themselves as

Scot, Jonas Keene, and Lucien Weatherby surveyed the damage on board the Osage.

"Take us a day, Jonas said, "to rig up a new mast, an' we won't find any hickory up this way."

"That means Brandon will pass us," Weatherby observed, "unless this storm damaged his boat too."

"No such luck." Jonas laughed grimly. "You'll see him movin' upriver in the mornin'."

There was little other damage to the Osage. Some of the deck boards had been loosened, but this could be easily repaired. The matter of the mast was something else.

In the light of the fires from the shore, Scot had the men clear away the broken mast. Romaine had his coffeepot over the flames, and they went ashore to eat as the stars were coming out.

Carole Du Bois, helping at the fire, handed Scot a tin cup full of coffee and a plate of beans and salt pork. She said, "Will the broken mast hold us up long, Scot?"

"Long enough to let Brandon get past us," Scot told her.

"He'll hurt you if he can, won't he?"

"He's tried to hurt us before." Scot smiled faintly. "I'm sure he was behind the fire we had, and he had someone cut our cordelle line halfway through as we were about to go through a bad stretch of water. He knows that if we get upriver and establish our posts we'll cut his trade in half, maybe more than half."

"Who do you think cut the cordelle line?" Carole asked him.

Scot shrugged. "We figured one of our own crew, but

119

we don't know which one. We've been watching them ever since."

"This man may try to hurt you again."

"I know." Scot nodded. "There's nothing we can do about it but watch every moment."

He saw Nanette watching them from across the fire as she ate. Her dark eyes seemed to be glowing in the fire-light. After a while she got up and went back on board the boat.

Scot said to Carole, "Do you get along with her?"

"She's quiet," Carole said, "but we don't have any trouble."

Scot had noticed that, also, about the vivacious Nanette La Rue. At the beginning of their trip Nanette had been as lively as a kitten, singing and chattering, but recently she'd become quiet, and this had started even before Carole came aboard. There was little doubt in Scot's mind that Nanette was not too pleased with another woman on the Osage, but that was not all of it. Something else was eating at Nanette, something he didn't understand.

Carole said thoughtfully, "You will be glad when you don't have women on your boat. It will be much easier for you."

"You're with us," Scot reminded her, "until we return next spring, and that's a long time." He watched her face as he sipped the coffee and he said, "What will you do? Will you go downriver?"

There was a shadow on Carole's face. "There is nothing downriver for me," she said. "I cannot live there."

"You should marry," Scot told her. "You should find a good man."

She said over her shoulder as she was going back to the fire, "Find one for me."

He smiled a little as he watched her bring Weatherby his supper, and then stop and talk with him for a while. He noticed that Weatherby treated her as he would a white woman. The artist was always the gentleman, always polite and courteous. He'd noticed, also, that Weatherby's eyes seemed to drift in Carole's direction quite often when they were on board or eating around the fire. He wondered what Weatherby, the cultured gentleman with fine background and education, thought about this French-Cheyenne girl.

He knew what *he* thought about her. He liked her very much, and he would have married her, but one thing held him back. There was always a picture in his mind of Nanette La Rue on the cargo-box of the Osage, her black hair blowing in the breeze, dressed in a white blouse and the bright red skirt she'd made of trade goods, and laughing, singing. At that moment she had seemed like the spirit of the river, this river he was trying to conquer.

There was another picture, too, of a small girl dressed in boy's clothes, wet and bedraggled, with hauntingly large eyes sitting on the steps in the Red Lion Tavern in St. Louis.

After eating Scot went aboard again to take another measurement on the mast they would need to cut on the morrow. He found Nanette sitting up in the bow, staring upriver, almost hidden in the shadows there. When he

121

went over to her she looked up at him, and then looked away again.

"You're not happy?" Scot asked her.

Nanette shrugged. "One is never happy for long," she told him.

"You were happy when we started on this trip," Scot reminded her. "Is it because Carole has come aboard?"

"Carole is good," Nanette said. "She has tried to be friendly."

"You don't like her?"

"I like her," Nanette said.

"But you've become very quiet. You don't laugh or sing any more since—" He stopped and he started to think back. "Since the night at the Ree village."

He remembered now that that was when it had begun. He'd kissed Nanette and he'd released her and gone ashore, and since that night she'd changed. He'd noticed it the next morning.

"I do not wish to laugh or sing," Nanette murmured, and she did not look at him as she said it.

"We will have to live together all winter," Scot told her, "in very dangerous country. We don't wish you to be unhappy, Nanette."

She looked up again, and this time she smiled. "You are a very good man," she said. "There is something I will tell you someday, Scot."

"Not now?"

She was not smiling any more. "Not now," she said dully. "I am not happy, Scot." She got up and she went hastily to the cabin, closing the door behind her.

Jonas Keene had come aboard, and he said to Scot

after Nanette had gone. "Wildcat's kind o' lost her claws lately, Scot."

"I know. Something bothering her, Jonas."

"One woman on board," Jonas observed, "an' you got heaven. Two, an' you got hell. That's the way it goes."

"Not this time," Scot said. "Something else bothering little Nanette."

"Better keep your mind on Carole," Jonas advised. "Somebody else is."

He glanced toward the shore, and Scot saw Lucien Weatherby still chatting with Carole Du Bois.

"Weatherby didn't go fer the Ree women," Jonas murmured, "but a part-French girl is somethin' different."

Scot didn't say anything to that. He wasn't sure whether he should feel pleased or displeased. These weeks on the Missouri he had learned to like and respect the artist, and Lucien Weatherby could find no better girl than Carole Du Bois—if he himself were not interested in her.

Immediately after breakfast the next morning, Scot left with Jonas Keene, Baptiste Privot, and several of the crew to find a tall pine to be used as a mast. They moved through the timber lining the river at this point, heading downriver, and as they came out into a clearing along the river they saw a boat being poled up along the east bank.

"Yellowstone Gal," Jonas Keene growled. "Brandon's makin' time. That storm never touched him, Scot."

Scot watched the Yellowstone Gal move slowly by them, the crew working the poles, moving up and down rhythmically along the catwalk. Cass Brandon was up on the cargo-box at the sweep. He didn't see them on the opposite shore of the river, and the keelboat moved by around a bend in the river.

"He'll be glad as hell to see us tied up at the bank," Jonas said grimly.

"We catch him," Baptiste said. "Pouf! Baptiste will pull the Osage with teeth."

"Hell of a lot o' good that will do," Jonas grunted. "Let's find that tree."

They found a straight pine a half hour later, the right size and thickness, and Baptiste cut it down in a few minutes. They trimmed off the branches and carried the pole back to the Osage, and set to work installing it in the bow.

Far upriver, they could see Brandon's keelboat moving around a bend, and Lucien Weatherby said, "He wouldn't even give us a horn as he went by.

"We catch him," Baptiste Privot repeated.

It took almost the remainder of the day to shave the mast to fit, and rig it up in the bow. At nightfall by the light of a shore fire they rigged up the sail and then put down their tools.

"Ready to go." Jonas nodded in satisfaction. "Wasn't too bad, but that mast ain't like the one we had."

"It'll get us where we're going," Scot said.

They were off again in the morning, poling away from the shore, Scot at the sweep and Baptist Privot in the bow with the pole. The river started to narrow here and became deeper, and they had to get out the oars. Then it was the cordelle line in the afternoon with the men stumbling along the west bank, sinking into mudbanks up to the knees, up to the waist, scrambling on, cursing, brushing away the clouds of mosquitoes they had disturbed in the marshes and sedgy grass.

It was going to be the line more than anything else, Scot knew as they progressed up the river. Occasionally the wind would help them, and now and then they could use the oars and the poles, but it was the line and the brute strength of the Creoles that did most of the work.

The tawny hills through which they had been moving in the Sioux country gave way to a wild, crazy, jumbled mass of peaks and battlements, palisade walls of red and yellow and white through which the brown river rolled, cutting new channels, caving in sandbanks.

The Creoles looked about fearfully as they poled through this weird land of ghosts and goblins, and the more fearful Blackfeet beyond. There was little talk, and when they had to go out with the cordelle line each man looked at the other, and Jonas Keene had to go ashore first with his long rifle to lead the way.

"They're afraid o' their own shadows," Jonas said in disgust. "Ain't no Blackfeet in these parts. Ain't any Injuns livin' in these rocks. This is land just flung away fer no purpose."

Nanette stared at the rock formations in awe, but Carole, who had come through here alone in a frail canoe on her way down from Fort Adams, was not overly impressed.

The high cliffs encompassed them on all sides. They pushed onward toward the higher mountains beyond, and the land was bleak and desolate. There was very little game here. It was a dry, dusty country that even the buffalo seemed to shun.

They camped at night on. a sandy island in the middle of the river, and they found Cass Brandon's campfires here, one day old, and a fresh mound of earth where one of his crew had been buried.

"Mountain fever," Jonas Keene said. "Hits 'em every once in a while. Or it could o' been a fight."

They came out of the wild land, and in two days slid the ,Osage up on the sandy bank below Fort Adams, where Carole Du Bois had lived.

The post was abandoned. The few half-breed clerks who had worked for Jacques Du Bois had run off, taking with them whatever furs Jacques had collected. The shelves of the big, roomy store were empty, too, indicating that all in the vicinity had helped themselves.

The Indians were gone. There were a few tepee poles standing, and the bare ground where tepees had stood. A half-wild dog roamed among the buildings, but no human beings appeared when Scot hailed the post.

They camped on the shore that night, and Scot walked with Carole to the little picket enclosure where her father had been buried. Her Cheyenne mother lay there, too, and Carole was very silent as she looked down at the two mounds of earth.

Scot walked to the edge of the hill overlooking the river where the two had been buried, and he watched the Creoles down below sprawled on the sand near the Osage. He was thinking that this was what had become of Jacques Du Bois, engage for the Empire Fur Company. In a little while the post would fall down. The

126

brush would cover these two mounds, and the Frenchman would be only a memory, leaving nothing behind him.

He didn't want to end that way. He had to leave his mark up here in the wilderness, even if that mark meant only a trail through to the Promised Land of the Columbia.

## *Chapter Eleven*

In three weeks after leaving Fort Adams they were in the foothills of the Rockies, the timber reaching down to the river, and game more abundant than Scot had ever seen it before. There were buffalo in the parks off the river, and antelope, and huge, stately elk moving through the trees. Giant grizzlies roamed along the river's edge, seeking berries and insects, and the Creoles feared them almost as much as the Blackfeet. The big bears were fearless, and a she-bear with a cub was something to be avoided.

"Best game country in the West," Jonas Keene told Scot. "Reckon you kin see why the Blackfeet don't want it spoiled."

"We won't spoil it for them," Scot said. "All we want from them is trade."

When Jonas went ashore now he found Indian sign, recent hunting camps, the bones of dead animals killed in the meadows off the river, and each day they became more wary.

They saw Cass Brandon's campfire smoke on occasions, and Scot hoped against hope that Brandon hadn't been able to get close to the Blackfeet with his whisky so that he could set them on the keelboat following him.

"Ain't likely that he will," Jonas observed. "Not if I know them Blackfeet. Reckon he'll have it as tough as we will."

They were very close to Brandon now, and once they even caught sight of the Yellowstone Gal far upriver, the crew at the poles. She was gone around a bend a few minutes later.

That same afternoon a half-dozen Blackfeet rode their ponies down to the water's edge on the west shore of the river and watched them steadily, silently, as they poled up along the east bank. Scot studied the Blackfeet thoughtfully. They were farther north now than any keelboat had ever gone before, moving deeper and deeper into the dangerous Blackfoot hunting grounds. The Indians here were not like some of the Plains tribes. The Blackfeet were rich, well fed, many of them carrying guns purchased from the British traders farther north. Unlike the tribes farther south, they did not depend wholly upon buffalo for meat. Here all game was plentiful, and could be found all the year round, whereas the buffalo drifted south in the winter, leaving the high plains bare and desolate.

"Look at them ponies," Jonas said admiringly. "Fat an' saucy like their riders, an itchin' fer trouble."

The Creoles on the catwalk eyed the Blackfeet riders with terror, almost afraid to look at them. The Indians sat astride their spotted ponies, a few of them carrying lances, the others with new rifles. One of them lifted his rifle as if to try to shoot, but then lowered it again, realizing that the distance was too great.

"Them fusils they carry won't go this far," Jonas said, "but I could drop any one of 'em with my long rifle at this distance."

Scot stood up on the cargo-box and lifted his hand to the Indians, palm toward them, a gesture of friendliness. The Blackfeet just looked at him, and after a while they turned their ponies back into the woods, crossed a meadow beyond, and disappeared.

That night they looked for an island upon which to camp, but were unable to find one, and reluctantly Scot turned in toward the west bank, finding a small cove, the entrance of which was fairly well concealed by high willows. Immediately guards were set out around the camp and a small cook fire was made.

Jonas Keene made a wide circuit of the area, and came back in a half hour to report that he'd seen nothing. "Safe enough fer tonight," he told Scot. "Injuns don't move about much after dark."

Scot watched Carole Du Bois and Nanette coming ashore, and then walking a short distance up along the river to wash. Carole nodded to him and smiled as she came across the plank. Nanette nodded too, but she did not smile, and Scot looked after her thoughtfully.

Jonas said, "Ain't the same gal came aboard back in St. Louis, Scot."

Scot shook his head. He watched them walk up along the curve of the bank, and then he went to the cook fire for his coffee and beans and elk steak from the animal Jonas had shot that morning.

Lucien Weatherby said as he came up, "That bunch

didn't look too friendly, Scot. Think we'll get close enough to them so that I can make a few sketches?"

Scot shrugged. "When we get our post set up and show them that we're here for trade, they may become more friendly. They've always resented white trappers coming in to work their streams. We won't be doing any trapping."

Weatherby nodded. "They were fine specimens," he said, his pale blue eyes gleaming. "The Blackfeet are lords of these mountains."

Carole came back to the fire, and Scot noticed that Weatherby got up to pour her coffee. She smiled as she thanked him, and the artist flushed slightly. He'd started to make a sketch of her in the evenings as they sat around the fire, and from the few glimpses Scot had had of the drawing, he'd noticed that Weatherby had exceeded himself. Carole was not too displeased with the sketch, either. She had held her hand up to her mouth, Indian fashion, the first time she had seen it, after Weatherby had been drawing for nearly an hour.

Scot packed his pipe after eating, and then he noticed that Nanette had not come up to the fire for her supper. He assumed she had gone aboard after Carole came back, intending to eat later, but when she did not come he wandered down toward the plank and the Osage, looking for her.

It was dark aboard the boat. He called softly, "Nanette."

When she did not answer he crossed the plank, walking down toward the cabin. It was dark inside and he bent down to call again, a little worried this time, and still she did not answer.

130

He stepped into the cabin, bending down inside because there was not sufficient room for him to stand upright. He said, "Nanette?"

When he struck a light he found that the cabin was empty. Up on deck again, he stared toward the shore and the little campfire. He could see shadowy figures around the fire, but Nanette was not there, nor was she on board the Osage. He made a quick survey of the bow and stern, and then crossed the plank rapidly.

Lucien Weatherby was getting out his sketch of Carole when Scot came ashore, and Carole was sitting on a rock near the fire where the firelight could play on her smooth, oval face.

"Where is Nanette?" Scot asked her.

Carole looked at him. "She didn't feel well and she told me she was going back on board."

"She's not aboard," Scot said.

Lucien Weatherby put aside his sketch. Jonas Keene tossed the dregs of his tin cup and set it down near the fire.

"Gone?" he asked.

Scot called sharply, lifting his voice so that it carried out into the dark forests all around them: "Nanette! Nanette?"

There was no answer. He called a little more loudly, and the Creoles gathered closer to the fire. One of them crossed himself, and Scot heard the murmur "*Les Pieds Noirs.*"

"Ain't no Blackfeet within a mile o' here," Jonas growled. "I been out. I know."

"Nanette?" Scot called again, and then he said to

131

Carole, "Where did you leave her?"

"She was washing up along the cove," Carole said. "When I waited for her to return with me she said that she was going aboard and would come in a moment."

"Ain't no place fer a woman to be wanderin' around," Jonas said gruffly. "No Blackfeet around now, but that ain't sayin' they ain't within hollerin' distance."

"Ask the guards if they've seen her," Scot said to the hunter, and then he moved up along the cove to the spot where the two girls had washed.

Carole and Lucien Weatherby went with him, and when they reached the place, less than thirty yards from the campfire, Carole said, "It was here. I thought she was coming behind me when I returned."

"She didn't come back," Scot muttered. He looked around on the ground when Weatherby came up with a burning faggot from the fire. He could see the footprints of the two girls at the water's edge, but there were no signs of a scuffle of any kind.

Jonas came up with the word that none of the three sentinels he had set back in the timber had seen Nanette. The hunter got down on hands and knees to study the ground in the light of the torch, and then he pointed toward the willows and he said simply, "She went that way. The gal never came back to the boat. She was wearin' shoes. They're easy enough to foller here."

"She went upriver?" Scot asked slowly.

"Around the bend o' the cove," Jonas explained, "keepin' in the willows. That's how our boy upriver didn't see her."

"Where would she go?" Lucien Weatherby asked.

"There's nothing upriver for her."

"Not much," Jonas Keene agreed. "Exceptin' Black-feet, an' mountains, an' Cass Brandon."

He tossed the faggot into the river and it sizzled out. The four of them stood in the darkness along the river. A screech owl whirled by them, and across the river they heard a crashing sound—the sound an elk or a bull moose would make coming down to the river to drink.

Scot said, "What does that mean, Jonas?"

"Ain't sure yet," Jonas said. "Ain't sure, either, that it was Gaston Diderot cut that cordelle line way downriver. Ain't sure about a lot o' things, Scot. There was a fire on board the Osage back at Leavenworth, an' the only one on board was Nanette La Rue. Right after that the cordelle line was near cut through, an' then Nanette kind o' took a walk in the woods once an' we never found out where she went. We was campin' right next to Brandon that time."

"She doesn't know Brandon," Scot said dully. "She's never seen him."

"We don't know that," Jonas told him. "She never came aboard this boat proper-like, Scot. What if she was workin fer Brandon from the beginnin', and he put her up to stowin' aboard to see what damage she could do fer him?"

Scot was thinking of the strange change in Nanette in recent weeks. He'd been trying to figure what had caused that. If what Jonas was saying was true, then Nanette had had a change of heart and was regretting that she'd consented to do Brandon's dirty work. It still seemed, however, to be a wild conjecture on Jonas

133

Keene's part, but what other reason would she have for leaving them here and going upriver at night in the direction of Brandon's camp, which could not be more than a few hours away? As Jonas had put it, there was nothing else upriver but Cass Brandon.

"What are you going to do, Scot?" Lucien Weatherby said sympathetically.

"Going after her," Scot told him. "We still don't know for sure that she's guilty. Jonas will go with me, and that will leave you in charge of the camp. We should be back before morning with news."

"Hope you find her," Weatherby said, "and I hope Jonas, here, is wrong."

"Hopin' that myself," Jonas Keene admitted, "but I been thinkin' a long time, an' that's the way the stick points."

Scot went aboard to pick up a rifle. When he came back he looked at Carole for a moment, noticing the puzzled expression on her face, and then he touched her arm lightly before walking off with Jonas.

He scarcely knew what to think of Carole tonight, but he knew that he had to find Nanette, who was now moving up along the river, alone, probably unarmed, in this dangerous Indian country. He had to find her and learn for sure that she had worked with Cass Brandon from the beginning, coming board the Osage at his instigation, deliberately to wreck the Osage if she could so that Brandon could work the upper-river trade alone. Brandon had had all winter back in St. Louis to formulate his plans, and there were women in a town like St. Louis who would go along with him on such a project, either for money or for something else, for love, for promises. Cass Brandon was expert at both.

He wondered if Nanette had known Brandon back in St. Louis, and perhaps been in love with the man, letting him persuade her that this was her opportunity to make a real fortune if he were able to garner the whole fur trade himself this summer. A girl very much in love with a handsome man like Brandon could conceivably go along with his schemes.

Jonas Keene said as they pushed through the trees along the river, "Ain't no use lookin' fer sign at night. We know which way she was goin'. Reckon she figured she could spot Brandon's campfire, an' she couldn't git lost if she stayed close to the river."

"We're fortunate," Scot said, "that there are no Blackfeet around."

"Not near our camp," Jonas told him. "Woods could be full of 'em farther upriver."

"They don't like to move about at night," Scot reminded him.

"Not unless they got a pretty damn good reason." Jonas laughed mirthlessly. "They'll do their fightin' in the mornin', but they'll get ready fer it at night if it's worth while."

"We'll hope they're not looking for a fight now," Scot murmured.

They pushed on up along the river, keeping it always in sight as they moved around marshland and willow thickets. Occasionally they frightened a deer as they moved through the woods, and the animal went crashing on ahead of them, to Jonas Keene's great disgust.

"Any Blackfeet along the river," he said, "an' they'll know somebody's movin'."

Scot listened attentively to a wolf howling across the river, making sure that it wasn't an Indian call. A fish jumped just off the shore, landing with a splash.

They had to cross several small streams that emptied into the Missouri, one of which was fairly deep, the water coming up to their waists, and Jonas said dryly, "She's havin' tough goin', but I reckon she's still ahead of us. We'd o' seen her otherwise." He added, "She's kind o' anxious to git where she's goin', an' she ain't wastin' time, either."

Scot didn't say anything to that, but he felt a little sick. He was beginning to realize that it was undoubtedly true that Nanette was running back to Brandon. She'd done the best she could for him, and now she was rejoining him.

"If she don't know," Jonas observed, "she'll find out soon enough the kind o' man he is. He'll treat her like a Ree squaw."

"We're still not sure she's going after Brandon," Scot said rather brusquely, and Jonas said no more on the subject.

They had been moving for nearly two hours through the woods, crossing meadows and parks, pushing their way through heavy thickets, and still they had seen nothing of the girl.

As they came out of another small stream, water streaming from them, Scot said, "We may have passed her while she was resting back in the brush."

"Still ahead of us," Jonas said.

"How do you know?"

"Marsh grass is wet here where she came out o' the stream," Jonas told him. "She crossed at this spot too. You kin feel the grass."

Scot had a picture of her stumbling along, near the point of exhaustion now, looking for that speck of reddish light that would be Cass Brandon's campfire. She would be imagining that every rustling leaf was a Blackfoot creeping up on her.

"Any Blackfeet come along the river in the mornin'," Jonas said glumly, "they'll see her sign sure as hell."

"She'll be at Brandon's camp long before morning," Scot told him, "unless we catch up with her."

"What do you figure on doin' with her if you catch her?" Jonas asked him.

Scot hadn't thought too much along those lines. "If she wants to go with Brandon, I can't stop her," he said, "but I have to be sure."

"She tried to burn your boat. She damned near wrecked it at the *embarras* downriver."

"I'd have to prove that," Scot told him.

Jonas just snorted, and they moved on upriver. It was rougher going along here, with a number of streams and creeks running into the river, some of them choked with willows, and the Missouri swinging back and forth around bends.

After an hour or so of this even Jonas had to stop. They crouched down in a small clearing, and Jonas said, "We could o' passed her now if she was restin' back there by some o' them creeks. If she was in the willows you could pass within five feet o' her an' not see her."

"I can call," Scot told him. "She might hear us."

Jonas Keene rubbed his nose and then spat. "Will she come?" he asked. "More likely you'll bring Blackfeet."

"Nothing to do but keep on till we hit Brandon's camp. It can't be too far ahead."

"Ever figure he might o' camped on the other side o' the river?"

Scot nodded. "Thought of that," he admitted.

"Reckon Nanette didn't," Jonas murmured, "unless she figured she could swim the river when she saw his camp, or call across fer him to get her."

They started up again, Jonas stepping into a shallow stream that emptied into a little cove. He was crossing the stream a few yards ahead of Scot when he stopped suddenly, motioned for Scot to wait, and then turned off at right angles toward the marsh grass. Something had caught his eye here in the darkness.

Moving about in the grass, which came nearly to his waist, Jonas called softly to Scot to follow. The water was cold, ankle-deep, and the bottom was muddy.

Scot pushed through the marsh grass, and then he saw the objects that had caught Jonas Keene's eye as he was going past the spot. They were large, round, dark mounds, almost hidden in the grass, about ten feet across.

"Bullboats." Scot muttered.

There were eight of the big oval boats that the upper river and Plains Indians made out of single buffalo hides stretched across willow frames, and then floated downstream. They were unwieldy affairs, spinning around and around in the water, but with the aid of long poles they could be used to go back and forth across the river, or down it for long distances.

Scot could see that the bottoms of these boats were still wet, indicating that they had been used that afternoon or evening, and had not had a chance to dry out.

"Blackfeet," Jonas Keene murmured, "an' they're up to somethin', if this hoss knows anything about 'em."

"Which way did they go?" Scot asked him.

Jonas worked his way up and down along the edge of the cove, and then he said, "They come out o' the marsh this side, which means they're headed upriver."

"After Brandon?" Scot wanted to know.

Jonas nodded. "These Injuns saw the Yellowstone Gal movin' up the river, an' they was on the other side. They crossed over in the bullboats maybe after dark, an' now they're workin' their way up to Brandon's camp, which they'll hit in the mornin'." He paused then, and he added significantly, "If this little gal, Nanette, is still lookin' fer Brandon, let's hope to hell she's behind us, an' not up ahead where them devils are."

## Chapter Twelve

They pushed on up along the river again, going very slowly now, knowing that any moment they were likely to walk right into the Blackfoot camp. A mile upriver Jonas stopped, motioning for Scot to wait behind. He moved up ahead by himself as Scot crouched down among the bushes along the edge of the water. Jonas disappeared as if he had been whisked away by a giant hand.

Scot waited, knowing that if there were Blackfeet in the vicinity, Jonas would find them without being seen himself. He was more concerned now about Nanette. If she were ahead of them she would certainly stumble into the Blackfoot camp. There was the possibility that they had already taken her, and had either killed her or were holding her prisoner before their attack on Brandon's camp. Knowing the Blackfeet, he hoped that if they had caught her they had already killed her. The thought of it made the sweat break out on his face even though the night was cool along the river. The smell of it came to him, dank and heavy, the smell of rotting vegetation along the bank. A nighthawk screamed downriver, and then he heard someone coming through the brush from that direction.

He waited, gripping the rifle in his hand, still crouching among the bushes. It was not an Indian coming toward him. An Indian would not make that much noise.

He started to rise from the brush as the figure came toward him, stumbling a little, weaving, and then he said softly, "Nanette."

She cried out sharply, but he was next to her in a moment, swinging an arm around her, putting the palm of his hand across her mouth to prevent her from making any other sounds. He said softly, "There are Blackfeet close by, Nanette. Don't make any noise."

She recognized him then, and she made no more sounds, but she was stiff in his arm, and then he released her. He said, "Sit down on the ground. Jonas has gone on ahead to look for the Blackfeet."

He squatted down beside her as she dropped to the ground wearily. He could hear her breathing heavily, and he realized that she was near to the point of exhaustion. He said nothing more, waiting until she recovered. In the deep shadows here he could not see her face. There was no moon, and here among the willows and the heavy brush even the stars did not help. He said finally, "We must have passed you back along the river. Did you see us, Nanette?"

"*Oui.*" Nanette nodded. "I lie in the brush. I see you go by."

"You didn't want us to see you?"

She didn't say anything to that, and Scot said slowly, "You're going up to Brandon's camp?"

Again she didn't speak, and he' knew then that it was true, and all that Jonas Keene had conjectured was true also.

"Where are the Blackfeet?" she asked.

"We found their bullboats back in the marsh," Scot told her. "They're headed upriver in the direction of Brandon's camp. Jonas feels they'll attack in the morning."

If she were Brandon's woman, this statement should have affected her. Scot waited for the reaction, but there was none. She sat down there on the ground in front of him, a small huddled shape like a little boy, and her head was down.

He said, "Why did you leave us, Nanette?"

"I have to run away," Nanette murmured, "I cannot stay by you."

"You are Brandon's woman?"

She did not speak immediately, and then Scot said to her, "I know that you fired the Osage back at Leavenworth, and that you cut through that cordelle line at the *embarras*. Why did you do it, Nanette?"

She did not answer, but he could see that she was shaking, and he heard the small sounds coming from her as she cried.

"I am bad woman," she sobbed finally.

"Do you love Brandon, or did he pay you to do it?"

"No—no money," Nanette cried. "I wouldn't do it for money. When he asked me to cut through the cordelle line I did not think you would be nearly killed. He did not tell me that. I wanted to wreck your boat so that you could not go anywhere. I would not kill you, Scot."

"All right," Scot muttered. "Start from the beginning. You met Brandon in St. Louis?"

"*Oui,*" Nanette whispered. "I meet him when I come up from New Orleans."

"That part of it is true?"

"I have been in St. Louis three months before I meet you. Brandon I meet on the boat up from New Orleans. I was not stowaway on New Orleans boat."

It was news to Scot that Cass Brandon had been down to New Orleans during the winter.

"He make love to me," Nanette went on. "He promise to marry me when he come back from upriver, but first he must have my help, he say. He tell me you are bad man who do him much harm years ago. You want to steal all furs upriver which belong to him."

"You told him you'd help him stop me, and then he'd marry you."

142

"He lie," Nanette sobbed. "He tell me you are bad, but he is bad. He try to have me kill you at the *embarras*."

"And now you are going back to him." Scot scowled.

"I cannot stay by you," Nanette explained dully. "I kill myself. I have done much wrong."

You think Brandon will want you?"

Nanette shook her head. "I cannot stay by you," she repeated, "and eat your bread. There is another girl, too."

"Were you supposed to rejoin Brandon somewhere upriver after you'd wrecked my boat?" Scot asked her. "Brandon say you will take me back to Leavenworth, or leave me at Fort Tecumseh. He find me there."

"He'd find another woman sooner than that," Scot grated. "I know him. It was his idea for you to hide aboard the Osage, and pretend that you had no home and no people?"

"I do not pretend," Nanette murmured. "It is true my people die back in New Orleans. I am alone. Brandon tell me to dress up in boy's clothes and follow you. I am to stay near you until the Osage leave St. Louis."

"That morning when we camped near Brandon you went ashore to see him, and he told you about the cordelle line. He knew we'd have to use the line through the *embarras*."

"*Oui*." Nanette nodded.

"You heard anything from him since?" Scot wanted to know. "Did you see him again?

"*Non*," Nanette said. "I think much. I think he is bad, man, and you are good. At Ree village I see you are good."

"Hell of a lot o' talkin' goin' on around here," someone said at Scot's elbow. "Don't you know them Blackfeet kin hear a leaf fall, Scot?"

Scot turned to look at Jonas Keene, who had slipped silently up next to them and was now squatting, Indian fashion, on the ground.

"What did you find?" Scot asked him.

"See *you* found somethin'," Jonas murmured. "I run into near a hundred Blackfeet camped half a mile below the Yellowstone Gal. Gittin' ready to hit in the mornin', I'd say." To Nanette he said dryly, "Reckon that's the bunch you was walkin' into."

Nanette didn't say anything to that, and Scot realized that in her present mood she didn't care. She hadn't been going back to Brandon; she had been going away from Scot, and there was no other place she could go up here in the wilderness. She had been fair in that respect.

"We'll have to warn Brandon," Scot said.

"Serve him damn right," Jonas growled, "if them Injuns took his hair. Reckon he'd never warn us, Scot."

"He's a white man," Scot murmured. "We can't let him be wiped out."

"Even if he's waitin' fer 'em," Jonas observed, "he stands a good chance o' losin' his hair. What about this gal? She goin' back to our camp?"

"She's going back," Scot said. "Nanette made a mistake." He saw Nanette look up at him quickly as he rose to his feet, and then he said to Jonas, "Think you can get into Brandon's camp without the Blackfeet seeing you?"

"Happens one o' his damn Creole guards put a bullet through me," Jonas said, "you'll know where I am."

144

"Keep your head down," Scot smiled at him, "and my respects to Brandon. Tell him to get his boat off the shore if he wants to keep it."

"Watch yourself on the way back," Jonas warned him. "Where you find one Blackfoot you're likely to find more. They come swarmin' like bluebottle flies when they smell blood."

"We'll be careful," Scot said.

When Jonas disappeared again into the shadows, he took Nanette's arm and turned downriver again. She went with him without a word, but when they had walked a dozen paces she stopped and said, "You want me to come back, Monsieur Scot?"

"Yes," Scot told her. "I went after you to bring you back."

"Why do you bring me back when I try to burn your boat?"

"We'll talk about it tomorrow."

"Now," Nanette persisted. "We talk about it now, Scot."

Scot looked down at her. "You want to know?" he asked softly, and then he reached forward and took her in his arms, drawing her to him. He held her tightly for some time, and then he bent down and kissed her, and he said, "There's your reason." He felt her shaking again as she started to cry, and he said, "We'll get back to the camp, Nanette. It's dangerous here."

"You love me?"

"I love you," Scot told her. He knew now where he stood, and this knowledge made him a free man again. It was all so very simple. He had always loved Nanette,

145

from the first moment he had seen her. Even when she had been dressed as a boy he had been peculiarly drawn to her. She had made her mistake, and it was over, and she knew that it had been a mistake.

Carole would find herself a good man. There were plenty of good men with the Empire Fur Company, and any one of them would be proud to have Carole.

"You are good man," Nanette said softly.

There was a faint movement on the water to Scot's left, a blur, and then he heard the swish of a pole. Grabbing Nanette, he threw her to the ground, falling down beside her, just as a bullboat slid in toward the shore, two dark shapes working the long poles.

Farther down along the river's edge, a second and a third and a fourth boat were coming in, dark forms stepping out of them into the water, dragging the boats up on the shore.

"Blackfeet," Scot whispered.

They were reinforcements for the group about to attack Brandon's camp upriver. He remembered Jonas Keene's warning then. This group had come from across the river, undoubtedly drawn by the prospects of booty and scalps.

Three more bullboats followed the first four, making seven in all. Two of the seven came in to shore above the spot where Scot lay with Nanette, the rest below them. They could move neither upriver nor downriver now, and they were so close to the bullboats that it was impossible to head away from the river, either, without being seen by the Blackfeet.

Tightening his grip on Nanette, Scot realized that their

only hope lay in remaining still in the high grass here, hoping that the Blackfeet wouldn't stumble over them as they started upriver.

He moved his right hand, sliding the hunting knife from his belt. The rifle lay on the ground beside him, a useless weapon with only one bullet in it. At least thirty additional Blackfeet had come across the river in the bullboats. It would be impossible to reload after firing that first shot, and Scot knew that if it came to a tussle he would have to depend upon the knife—for the Blackfeet, and for Nanette La Rue if it became apparent that he had no chance to break out of this encirclement.

He could hear Nanette breathing very fast as she lay beside him watching the Indians coming out of the boats, paddling along the sandy shore, dragging the boats back deeper into the high grass. One of them came within ten feet of them, and for one moment Scot thought the Blackfoot would continue and step directly on them. He changed his direction, however, and passed six or eight feet to their left.

They could hear the low guttural voices, and Scot caught the smell of them, always distinct and unpleasant at close quarters—the rank smell of unwashed bodies and wood smoke, and the blood of animals, and grease.

All the boats were stowed back in the high marsh grass now, and the Blackfeet were assembling at a spot a dozen yards downriver from where Scot and Nanette lay. Another Indian coming down from the bullboat above them passed within five feet of them, and Scot could feel Nanette's body tighten under his arm. He gripped the bone handle of the knife, ready to spring to his feet, but the Blackfoot went on, not seeing their dark shapes on the. ground.

"If they stumble on us," Scot whispered in Nanette's ear, "we'll make a run for the river. Can you swim?"

"*Non*," Nanette murmured.

Scot didn't say anything to that. He knew it would have to be the knife now if the Blackfeet closed in on them. The thought of sliding it into her body made him sick, but the other alternative was a thousand times worse. Nanette was not a Cheyenne girl who could take care of herself among Indians. She was white.

A conference was taking place down along the shore. They could hear the talk, and even occasionally a low, mirthless laugh, and the sound of it went through Scot. Indians did not laugh in the presence of white men, and he had never heard one laugh before. They laughed tonight, contemplating the murder of twenty-five or thirty-odd men in Brandon's encampment. When they had destroyed Brandon's boat and crew, they would come after his.

They started to straggle up along the shore in the direction of the first Indian party, and they walked between Scot and the river, a strip of land not more than fifteen yards wide.

Lifting his head slightly, Scot watched them, their tall dark shapes outlined against the starlight, naked to the waist, an occasional eagle feather protruding from the long, braided hair. The beads and bracelets they wore rattled softly as they went by, and he could hear their light footsteps in the squashy earth. One Indian stopped and squatted down almost within arm's length of them

148

to adjust a moccasin string, and then went on again.

Scot watched them, the Green River knife tight in his fist, ready to spring. Now only a half dozen of the thirty were still below them, down near the bullboats. Four of the six came on together in a group, and then a fifth man swung out, passing to the right of Scot and Nanette. The last man lingered behind as he pulled one of the bullboats farther back into the high grass. Then he came on after the others had moved up beyond Scot, and he walked directly toward their place of concealment.

Nanette let out a small sound, so very faint that even the Blackfoot coming toward them did not hear it. Scot drew one knee forward slowly, gently. He got his hands on the ground, the palm of the left hand flat, and the other with the knuckles to the ground, holding the knife.

There was still the faint possibility that the Indian coming toward them would change direction at the last moment, but he didn't. His shape grew bigger and bigger as he advanced. He was a tall man, wiry, with sloping shoulders. His chest was naked, but he wore high leggings, and there was a feather in his hair. A bow was slung across his shoulder. He would have a knife and possibly an ax in his belt. Scot made a mental note of these two weapons, and then as the Blackfoot came up to them, pausing when he saw the dark shapes on the ground directly in front of him, the grass parted by their bodies, Scot sprang at him.

His left hand caught the Indian around the throat, choking off the cry of alarm that started there. His head and shoulders rammed into the Blackfoot, driving him backward through the tall grass.

As they both went down in the grass, Scot drove in the knife, swinging it up into the Indian's side. It went in smoothly, easily, and he heard the Blackfoot gasp and murmur as if in protest.

He lay on top of the man, still clutching his throat so that he could not cry out. The Indian struggled a little, trying to unseat him, but the strength was ebbing from his body, and in a little while he was still.

Scot was rolling off when he heard the low call of one of the Blackfeet who had gone on ahead. This man apparently had been waiting for the loiterer, and he may have heard the sound of their falling bodies on the ground.

Scot crouched in the grass, seeing this second man materialize out of the shadows ahead, coming back slowly. He stopped and called again, softly, but a little more alert now.

Nanette had got up on hands and knees when Scot charged the first Blackfoot. Scot saw her sink down again, and then he rose to his feet and started to walk directly toward the second Indian, the bloody knife steady in his hand.

He walked without hesitation, hoping the Blackfoot wouldn't realize that it wasn't the man he was expecting until it was too late. He saw the Indian standing there in a patch of deeper shadows made by the trees behind him.

The man carried a gun. Scot caught the dull, metallic gleam of the barrel in the starlight. He walked on, gripping the knife, pushing through the marsh grass. When he was within six feet of the Indian, he suddenly charged, coming in low again, and then he brought the knife in and down, a swinging overhand motion, plunging it down into the Blackfoot's chest.

The knife point skidded off bone this time, but went on, and the Indian staggered back, letting out an agonized cry as he fell.

Scot rolled over on top of him. Whipping the knife out of the man, he sprang to his feet and raced back to where he had left Nanette. The Blackfeet up ahead of him were bounding back now, and he could hear their low, animal cries and the padding of their moccasined feet.

Scooping up his rifle with one hand and yanking Nanette to her feet with the other, he plunged on in the direction of the bullboats. When he reached the nearest one he stumbled over a pole that had been dropped in the grass.

Snatching it up, he handed it to Nanette and pushed her in the direction of the river.

"Hurry," he whispered.

Overturning one of the light, circular boats, he dragged it rapidly down into the shallow water, pushed Nanette into it unceremoniously, and kept driving it out into the water, careless of the sounds he made now, knowing that they had been seen.

A fusil roared from the bank when he was thirty or forty feet from the shore in knee-deep water. He heard the ball whistle past him, and then several arrows followed. The Blackfeet were yelling in excitement, running down along the bank as Scot tumbled into the bullboat and took the pole from Nanette.

"Get down," he ordered, and he pressed her to the bottom of the boat with one hand as he dug the pole into the river bottom with the other.

The bullboat was revolving gently, slowly, the current beginning to catch it. Scot dug in desperately with the pole, driving it farther out into the river.

He could see the Blackfeet dragging several of the bullboats down to the water, also, and he thought dryly of Jonas Keene's observation that the Blackfeet did not like to fight at night. No Indian cared to fight at night, but if a fight was enjoined, they did not run away from it.

More arrows were coming, whispering around him, and he heard one of them rip through the skin of the boat just below his waist. He was out in deep water now, and his pole was scarcely touching bottom. The current had him and they were moving at a fairly fast rate. The shadows on the river made them difficult to see, and a hard target to hit.

He could make out four boats coming out from the shore, several Blackfeet in each of them. Handing the pole to Nanette, he reached for his rifle, which he had dropped on the bottom of the boat, and lining the muzzle on the group of dark shapes in the lead boat coming after them, he squeezed the trigger.

There was a sharp yell from the lead boat. As one of the Blackfeet went down, the boat started to rock violently, eventually overturning and spilling the three remaining Indians into the water.

Calmly Scot knelt on the bottom of his own bullboat and reloaded the rifle. He said to Nanette, "You all right?"

*"Oui,"* Nanette murmured. "It is all right, Scot."

"Current will take us right back to our own camp," Scot told her. "Worst is over."

The remaining three bullboats were still coming after them, and the Blackfeet along the shore were moving parallel with them, sending occasional arrows in their direction, but they were far out in the river now, the full, strong current of the Missouri driving them.

Scot sent another rifle bullet back at the pursuing Blackfeet in the boats, and he said to Nanette, "These shots should put Weatherby on his guard when we come near the encampment. We'll make very good time going down with the current."

"We are safe now?" Nanette asked him.

"Yes," Scot said, trying to put conviction into his voice, "but keep down low. They may still shoot a few arrows."

The voices of the Blackfeet along the shore died away as they were left behind, but the three bullboats, containing nine or ten Indians, still came on, anxious to pick up a few scalps.

They don't know about the Osage downriver, Scot thought. This bunch came up late.

He reached down with the pole, tried to touch bottom and couldn't, and then drew the pole in again. He figured that in less than an hour, moving at this rate, they would be back at the Osage encampment. Lucien Weatherby would undoubtedly have heard the sound of the shots reverberating down the river, and he would be watching for trouble.

They had left Jonas Keene behind them, but Scot

wasn't worrying about the mountain man. Jonas could take care of himself in the woods as well as any Indian, and he would join up with them in due time after having warned Brandon.

"They are still coming after us," Nanette said, looking back at those three shadows on the river.

"They can't move any faster than we do in deep water," Scot told her, "and they're in for a surprise when they come down to the Osage."

There were no sounds from the Blackfeet in the bullboats. They were lean timber wolves on a trail now, eager and anxious for blood, knowing that the odds were on their side. If the current pushed Scot's boat in toward the shore again, and it lodged against a river bend or an *embarras,* the Blackfeet would have them. The Indians held to this hope, and they would follow on all through the night and the next day, the way wolves ran down an old bull on the open plains.

The first gray light was coming into the eastern sky as the bullboat rounded a sharp bend in the river, and Scot caught sight of the cove opening into which the Osage had been pushed the previous night.

He felt with his pole again, but it was still too deep here to touch bottom, and he had to smile a little at the impracticability of these bullboats. They were intended to drift, and to drift only. If a man wanted to get ashore he had to hope the current swung him in close enough so that he could use his pole, or he had to swim with it, dragging his light, clumsy boat behind him as best he could.

They saw the tall mast of the Osage above the low trees fringing the entrance to the cove, and then a man

154

came out on the promontory to stare at them as they drifted up. White river mist swirled around him as he stood on the point, and then as the mist lifted slightly, Scot recognized him as Baptiste Privot. Looking back upriver, he saw that the three pursuing bullboats were several hundred yards behind them, and that they had neither gained nor lost ground.

Lifting his voice, Scot called sharply, standing up in the boat so that Baptiste could see him. A flight of ducks in V formation winged far overhead, honking as they went north upriver. A curlew was calling from the far bank of the river, and then a coyote barked in the distance.

Baptiste disappeared, returning in a few moments with a coil of rope. Lucien Weatherby and several of the crew came with him. Baptiste waded out into the water until it came to his waist before he tossed the rope.

Scot caught the line, and then pointed behind him. The three Blackfoot bullboats were just sweeping around the bend of the river.

"Swivel gun," Scot called to Weatherby, and the artist nodded, running back toward the Osage.

Baptiste hauled in the bullboat, dragging it into the shallow water, and then he stopped to shake a big fist at the three helpless bullboats drifting along out in midriver, the huddled shapes of the Blackfeet in them. It was too deep for the Indians to pole, and they could do nothing but drift past the mouth of the cove where the Osage was half concealed.

As Scot lifted Nanette from the bullboat, several arrows came at them. He carried her in among the trees rapidly, and when they were inside the cove he saw Weatherby up in the bow of the Osage, lining the four-pounder on the target.

As the first bullboat slid past the cove entrance Weatherby let go with the first shot. The ball raised a geyser a few yards above the drifting boat.

The roar of the little gun silenced the Blackfeet, who had started to yell. They stared in the direction of the Osage, which they could now see clearly in the cove.

Two crewmen reloaded the four-pounder, and once again flame and black smoke belched from the muzzle, the boom of it rolling across the river, bouncing off the near hills.

The shot went home this time. The lead bullboat seemed to jump in the water. There were three Blackfeet in the boat. Two of them were spilled from the boat as if a big hand had slapped them. One man went into the water, and the second hung over the side of the boat as it bent down that way, slowly overturning.

The third Blackfoot swam frantically for the opposite shore. Scot, watching, saw a hand lift out of the water near the overturned bullboat, the fingers flexing, and then the hand disappeared. The round boat, bottom up now, river water making a glisten in the early-morning light, moved on down the river.

The two bullboats behind the first one quickly emptied as the Blackfeet hit the water and swam like so many beaver for the other shore. The Creoles cheered lustily.

Scot, walking along the sandy shore with Nanette La Rue, saw Carole watching from the cargo-box of the keelboat. She looked down at him speculatively.

156

## Chapter Thirteen

An hour after Scot had landed his bullboat at the cove, the Osage was being poled out of the cove, headed upriver. Nanette had gone into the cabin, and Carole was with her.

Lucien Weatherby listened with interest as Scot told him of their encounter with the Blackfeet after finding Nanette.

"We'll watch for Jonas along the shore," he said. "He'll be looking for us."

"You think they attacked Brandon's camp?" Weatherby asked, and Scot noticed that he asked no questions concerning Nanette.

"Brandon must have heard the shots," Scot told him. "If they hit him, it wasn't a surprise attack."

Weatherby, at the sweep handle, watched the river as the Creoles sat down at the oars after poling the keelboat out of the cove. He said thoughtfully, "This attack may make it difficult to set up a fort and bring in trade furs."

Scot shook his head. "This band are undoubtedly Bloods. We figured on doing most of our trading and setting up our posts deeper in the Blackfoot country—the land of the Piegan Blackfeet."

"The Piegans are the ones I want to paint," Weatherby said. "They're the true Blackfeet, aren't they?"

"The Siksika are actually the true Blackfeet, but the Piegans are much the same. The Piegans will fight, but they're not so crazy about war as the Bloods. The

157

Bloods look for trouble, where the Piegans may come for trade goods."

"That bunch we saw the other day," Weatherby said. "They could have been Piegans."

Scot nodded. "They'll be watching us. If we start to set out traps they'll be after us. This is their hunting land. Every animal in it belongs to them, and they'll fight us to the last man."

He saw Carole coming out of the cabin, and when he moved up to the bow she came to him there, and she said, "Nanette told me why she ran away last night."

Scot looked across the water. "I had to bring her back," he said.

"I know. I've seen that in your eyes for some time, Scot. She made a mistake, but she'll be a fine woman. She has courage."

"The Blackfeet didn't scare her too much," Scot replied.

"I'll try to help her while we're up here," Carole told him. "This isn't her country."

Scot considered that fact for a moment. "It's my country," he said.

"She will make it her country," Carole said. "She's that kind of girl. You have nothing to worry about. I'm happy for you, Scot."

Scot looked at her. "I wish as much for you," he said, and then he glanced up in the direction of Lucien Weatherby on the cargo-box, and he saw the artist watching them. Carole Du Bois just smiled and went back to the cabin.

An hour after they pulled out of the cove they saw

Jonas Keene standing on a promontory, motionless, waiting for them to catch sight of him. Another man in buckskin sat on the rocks beside him, smoking a clay pipe, and when he stood up, dwarfing Jonas Keene by his great bulk, Scot recognized the man immediately. The hair underneath his coonskin cap was flaming red, and as long as an Indian's. It was reputed that a half-dozen mountain tribes coveted that scalp, ranking it worth a dozen other scalps.

"Bearpaw Mike Malone," Scot said to Weatherby as the artist turned the Osage in toward the promontory. "You've heard of Mike, Weatherby?"

"Who hasn't?" Weatherby grinned. "I've sat at many of his campfires and listened to many of his tall tales, the greatest in the West. He's far from his usual haunts this time."

Bearpaw Mike Malone's buckskins were blackened and grease-stained. Most of the fringe was gone from his leggings. He carried the same kind of long rifle as Jonas Keene had, and Scot knew that he was just as adept with it. A buckskin pouch containing his possibles was slung over his shoulder, and a blanket, rolled and tied, was on his back.

"He's on foot," Scot said, "which means the Blackfeet got his horses."

"That looks like a fresh scalp in his belt," Weatherby commented. "He didn't do too badly himself."

The two hunters stepped out into the water as the Osage edged in toward the rocks. They came aboard, the Creoles eying the big redhead admiringly. He was as big and as broad in the shoulders as Baptiste Privot himself.

159

Baptiste knew him well, and the two giants capered around each other, slapping backs, poking, grinning, hitting each other with blows that would have downed ordinary men.

"Me, Baptiste," the Creole boasted, "with the bare hands I pull down trees. The *embarras*—"

"King o' the river, are you?" Bearpaw Mike grinned. "I'll roll you tonight, bucko. This hoss will turn you upside down, Baptiste."

"*Non!*" Baptiste roared. "Baptiste stronges' man in Northwes'."

"Hell with you," Mike Malone chuckled, and he went over to shake hands with Scot and then with Lucien Weatherby. To Weatherby he said, "Still drawin' pictures, Weatherby? Come to the wrong place this time, I'm thinkin'. Blackfeet'll rip your tongue out, fry it, an' then make you eat it. I know 'em."

"We'll see," Weatherby smiled. "How are you, Mike?"

"Tolerable," Bearpaw Mike said, "considerin' the varmints got off with three hosses and two packs o' prime beaver."

"You didn't do too badly," Weatherby said, nodding toward the new scalp at Mike's belt.

"Only one of 'em." Big Mike chuckled. "Got four on 'em, but they was rushin' me, near a thousand of 'em, an' this was the only hair I was able to take."

"Bloods?" Scot asked him.

"Allus the Bloods," Mike Malone said. "Piegans ain't botherin' you much if you stay away from their stampin' grounds."

"Where did you pick up the beaver?" Scot asked.

"Other side o' the mountains," Mike told him. "Just come down through snow six feet deep. I was clean back beyond the Flathead country. Damn Bloods jumped me seven—eight days back. I been pinchin' 'em a little when you boys came along."

Jonas Keene said to Scot, "You git back with the little gal?"

Scot nodded toward the cabin. "Another bunch jumped us after crossing the river. Had to make a run for it in one of their bullboats. You hear the shots?"

"Heard 'em," Jonas said, "an' had me worried a mite, you with that gal to take care of."

"What about Brandon?" Scot asked him. "You see him?"

"Told him to git to hell back into his boat." Jonas smiled. "He wasn't quick enough."

Scot stared at the tall hunter. "Blackfeet hit him?"

"Got his boat," Jonas said. "Brandon figured he'd make a stand on the shore. Some o' them Bloods swam to his boat, got aboard, an' killed the guards. They set fire to it while the shootin' was goin' on along the shore. She burned right down to the water's edge."

"Serves him right," Bearpaw Mike Malone growled. "Never had no use fer Brandon. He'll pat you on the back with one hand an' slip a knife into your ribs with the other."

"I skipped out after the fightin' started," Jonas said, "an' then ran into Mike along the river. Brandon didn't lose many men, but he ain't got a boat, an' his supplies an' trade goods is gone."

161

Two hours later the Osage moved past the spot where Brandon's Yellowstone Gal lay along the shore, still smoldering, a charred skeleton of a boat. Brandon and his crew were nowhere to be seen.

"You sure the Blackfeet didn't get him?" Scot asked.

"We saw that bunch crossin' the river in their bullboats this mornin'," Bearpaw Mike explained. "Brandon was tryin' to git what supplies he could out o' his keelboat afore she went under. They was satisfied with burnin' the boat."

"He'll have a time getting downriver again," Lucien Weatherby observed, "but there's plenty of game at this time of the year."

"Ain't worryin' about him." Jonas grinned. "Reckon he had it comin' to him, Weatherby."

Several hundred yards above the spot where Brandon had camped, in a small clearing along the river's edge, they saw a group of men watching them silently. Scot, at the tiller handle, immediately spotted Brandon's tall form and blond hair in the middle of them.

"Moved their camp," Jonas Keene said. "Reckon Brandon's worried about another Injun attack, an' he picked a better spot to defend himself." Looking at Scot, he said, "You goin' in?"

Scot nodded and turned the Osage in toward the shore. The Creoles rowed in slowly, and Brandon came down to the water's edge. He stood there alone, waiting for them.

"I'd be careful of 'em," Jonas warned Scot. "He's licked, but he ain't down yet."

Two of Brandon's Creoles caught the tie ropes, wrapping them around nearby trees, holding the Osage in place. Scot went over the side into the shallow water and up on the bank.

It was the first time he'd seen Cass Brandon since the fight, and he noticed that the blond man still carried a few small scars on his face from that encounter. His face was browned from the hot sun on the river, and his light hair was even a shade lighter. He was big and bland as ever as he watched Scot coming out of the water. He said then, "Obliged to you for sending Keene down to warn me last night."

Scot shook his head. "Didn't do too much good. They got your boat."

"We have our hair," Brandon said. "I can always get another boat—downriver." There was the slightest hesitation between the last two words, and then Brandon said carefully, "We're heading downriver tomorrow. Figured we'd build a few flatboats. Better than trying it overland."

Scot nodded. "How many men you lose in that fight?"

"Only three," Brandon told him. "We were lucky."

Scot had a look at the Yellowstone Gal's crew along the shore. Some of them squatted around an almost dead cook fire. The others lay on blankets, watching them. There were over thirty men in the crew.

"We're short coffee and beans," Cass Brandon was saying. "I have money to pay for a few sacks."

"Pay the company in St. Louis," Scot told him. "Money's no good up here."

He ordered Baptiste Privot to bring up the necessary sacks from the hold. The sacks were dumped on the

163

shore, and then Scot turned to go. He knew that he should be feeling bitter toward this man who had tried to wreck their boat, and who had nearly killed them, but Brandon was licked already. The loss of his keelboat was a big blow to the Great Western Fur Company, and it might mean the end of Brandon as a trader on the Missouri. A bourgeois was seldom given the opportunity to lose two keelboats and valuable cargos.

"Luck," he said briefly. "Watch the Sioux when you get farther downriver."

"They won't take us again," Brandon told him. He looked beyond Scot at the Osage, and Scot wondered if he were looking for Nanette, who was still in the cabin.

Scot said evenly, "She's going upriver with us."

Cass Brandon's lips parted in a grin, revealing his white teeth. "Who?" he asked.

Scot just smiled at him, stepped around the sacks on the beach, and waded out into the water again. Brandon and his crew were still watching from the shore as the Osage was rowed out into the middle of the river.

"He's a bad one," Bearpaw Mike Malone growled. "Reckon I'd o' put some wolf bait in them sacks, Scot."

"Glad to see him goin' the other way now," Jonas Keene said. "Reckon we'll have enough trouble with the Blackfeet as it is without somebody tryin' to make it worse fer us."

They moved out of sight of the silent group on the beach, and as they did so, Nanette La Rue came out of the cabin. Bearpaw Mike Malone, who had not been aware of her presence on the Osage, stared in amazement.

"Two women on board a keelboat," he muttered. "Hell's bells! How'd you git so far, Scot?"

Scot smiled down at Nanette. She was hesitant this morning, still worried after the revelation of the preceding night, not sure that she was being accepted.

"Ain't a bad looker, either." Big Mike grinned.

"Came aboard as a boy," Jonas Keene told him.

Scot watched Carole Du Bois go over and talk with Nanette, and then he saw Nanette look downriver toward the beach where they had left Cass Brandon and his crew. He wondered what she was thinking. Brandon undoubtedly had had a strong hold on her to persuade her to fire another man's boat. Was that hold entirely broken?

For one moment doubt and jealousy swept over Scot, and then they were gone. He remembered that last night Nanette had left him because she loved him, and didn't want to hurt him any more. She had walked out of his camp in Blackfoot country.

Sitting up on the cargo-box, Jonas Keene was saying to Mike Malone, "You figure on stayin' with us this winter, hoss?"

"Nothin' doin' downriver fer me," Bearpaw Mike told him. "If Scot kin use another hand, I'm your man."

"We can use you," Scot said.

"Kind o' owe them Bloods somethin', too." Mike grinned. "They'll be givin' you more trouble."

"Rather worry about the Bloods than a rival fur boat behind us," Jonas told him.

"We can forget about Brandon," Lucien Weatherby put in. "He made his gamble with the Indians, and he lost."

Scot, at the sweep, watched the river, moving the Osage up along the west bank. The Missouri was twisted and bent like a rope cast carelessly on the ground. It moved north and then cut west, and then capriciously swung down toward the south again, making huge bends so that they almost doubled upon themselves, and were hours making a few short miles over which a man could walk leisurely.

They saw no more of the band that had struck at Brandon, but once during the afternoon they spotted a group of a dozen Indians running a few buffalo across a park off the river, and Jonas Keene labeled them Blackfeet.

"Damn country's swarmin' with 'em," he growled.

They camped that night on a sandspit running out into the river, and Scot set a heavy guard ashore to prevent an attack from the land. Both Jonas Keene and Bearpaw Mike Malone slipped into the brush, making their way north and south along the river to scout for Indians.

Lucien Weatherby said as he stuffed his pipe and stretched his legs on the sand, "Should be thinking of settling in pretty soon, shouldn't we, Scot?"

"Few more days," Scot told him.

"You won't take a keelboat much farther than this," Weatherby said. "River's getting more shallow every day. The men used the poles most of the afternoon."

Scot nodded. "We're already farther north than any keelboat has ever come before," he said. "It's a new river. He watched Weatherby stop by the fire to get a coal for his pipe, and he had the feeling that the artist had something else to say, but was hesitant about getting around to it.

"Glad you were able to get Nanette back," Weatherby said.

Scot smiled a little. "I'm marrying Nanette," he said, "at the first opportunity."

Weatherby glanced at him quickly. "I thought it might be Carole," he murmured. "You've known each other a long time."

"I'm fond of Carole as a friend," Scot told him. "I think that's the way it will always be with us."

Weatherby was smiling now. "I have been at the courts of kings," he stated, "and I have never met a girl with more poise or more loveliness than Carole Du Bois. You have no objections if I pay more attention to her in the future?"

"No objections." Scot laughed.

"The fact that she is half red," Weatherby went on, "is of no consequence to me, and I don't believe it was to you."

"If she were the woman for me," Scot said, "I would have married her, even if she were all red."

"I intend to remain in this part of the country the rest of my life," Weatherby was saying. "I believe I could find no better wife to accompany me on my journeys. A white girl wouldn't find this gypsy life acceptable."

"You're wise," Scot said. He watched Carole coming toward them, and then he saw Nanette sitting on the cargo-box roof, watching the activity on the shore. He went aboard then and sat down next to her, seeing the quick smile of pleasure come to her face.

"I cannot see you all day," she said. "You are so busy, *mon cher.*"

"We won't be busy all the time," Scot told her. "Soon we'll stop and build our trading post."

Nanette nodded. "What did Monsieur Brandon say?" she asked, not looking at Scot.

"He doesn't know you," Scot said.

Nanette looked at him. "He lies," she said simply.

"I know," Scot agreed.

"I do not want to see him again."

"You'll never see him," Scot assured her. "He's heading downriver with his crew. The Blackfeet burned his boat."

"I am glad. He is bad man."

They watched Lucien Weatherby and Carole Du Bois strolling side by side up along the sandspit, and Nanette said, "You do not love her, Scot?"

"I love you," Scot said. "I never loved her."

"That is good," Nanette murmured. "I am so happy, *mon cher.*"

"Just the beginning of it," Scot told her, and then he saw her glance downriver again, and that faint, vague doubt came to him. Was she still thinking of Brandon? Had she come back to him only because he had gone after her?

## Chapter Fourteen

It was mostly the cordelle the next four days as they pushed on up the headwaters of the Missouri, and each day Scot examined the banks carefully, trying to decide upon the location of this first trading post and fort.

Much had to be taken into consideration in making the decision. They had to be near fresh water, which meant a stream running into the river; they needed open meadows beyond as grazing land for the stock that would be coming up later, or purchased from the Indians. They needed timber for the construction of the post and for firewood. If possible, an elevation was desirable.

Jonas Keene said to Scot, "You ain't gettin' all o' those things anywhere, Scot. You git one an' you lose the other. We need timber an' we need grass close by. Rest of it we kin do without."

The water was so low in the river now that they were able to pole even out in mid-river. Sand bars and shoals constantly held up progress, and the Creoles had to go ashore with the line and pull while the poles were manipulated aboard, literally dragging the Osage forward.

At noon five days after they left Brandon, Scot found the place for which he was looking. It was on a bend of the river with some protection on three sides. Heavy stands of cottonwood and mountain ash ran back fifty yards from the river. Beyond on the slopes the pines ascended toward the heights.

There was an enormous meadow just beyond the fringe of timber, and Scot had a look at it from the cargo-box roof as they poled in slowly toward the shore. The vista was tremendous. They could see miles toward the east and north, open country dotted with buffalo and elk, a few streams running through it

169

fringed with cottonwood and willow.

As they came in toward the shore, the marshes came alive with wild ducks and geese lifting up into the air, honking, fluttering toward the south. A big she-bear lumbered upriver, followed by two cubs. 1t was a silvertip, the giant grizzly of the mountain country.

"This is it," Scot said softly. He pointed with his finger toward an elevation about a hundred yards back from the river. "That will be the site of the post."

Bearpaw Mike Malone said succinctly, "Best damn game country I ever seen."

"We'll have a look around this afternoon," Scot said. "I want to go upriver a way and see what lies beyond."

"New country to me," Jonas Keene said. "Main trappin' grounds are due south from here. Maybe the Hudson Bay Company's been sendin' traders down this way, but none of 'em had the guts to stay around. Man kin lose his hair quick as a wink up this way."

The Osage ground up on the sand, several of the crew going into the shallow water with the tie ropes. Jonas Keene and Mike Malone moved away into the woods to make a brief survey of the surrounding territory before they made camp. Both men carried their rifles loaded as they melted into the woods.

Lucien Weatherby said to Scot as they waded through the shallow water and the marsh grass, "It's a good spot. You probably couldn't take a keelboat much farther north anyway, and in low water you'd never get her down again."

"I'll leave you in command this afternoon while we go upriver," Scot told the artist.

"We'll keep a close watch."

Jonas Keene and Bearpaw Mike came back in a half hour with the report that they had seen no fresh Indian sign.

"Plenty o' bones," Jonas observed, "layin' in the meadow. Blackfeet done a lot o' hunting in these parts, but they ain't along this part o' the river."

"Keep the fire low," Scot told Romaine, "and not too much smoke. We won't advertise the fact that we're here until we get up a few temporary barricades."

Scot ordered Nanette and Carole to remain on board the boat after eating, and then with Jonas Keene and Bearpaw Mike Malone he started up along the river.

It was good to be afoot again after so many days on the river, and the three of them swung through the woods, coming out into the park beyond. They skirted the timber then, moving north with it along the river.

Unintentionally, they frightened a small herd of buffalo grazing in a hollow ahead of them, and the buffalo lumbered out of the indentation and headed across the park.

Jonas Keene frowned and said, "That ain't good. Anybody's watchin' off in that open country, they see buffler movin' fast downwind, they'll know somethin's scared 'em."

"Keep a sharp eye," Mike Malone said. "Only way to keep your hair."

They went back into the timber now, noticing how it had thinned out along here, in places the meadows running directly down to the water's edge, and the banks broken with buffalo trails. The river was choked with small islands and sand bars, making navigation virtually impossible.

Dense clouds of wild ducks and geese whirled up into the air. Big mule-tail deer came down to drink on the opposite bank, looked at them stupidly for a moment, and then lunged back in among the trees.

They pushed on over the ridge, coming down through pine timber, and then they saw the abandoned camp of an Indian band. A few lodgepoles still stood on the spot. There was a burial ground beyond, scaffolds standing among the trees, the bodies of the dead probably picked clean by the birds.

"Dead Blackfeet don't hurt none." Bearpaw Mike grinned. "Live ones I'm worryin' about."

Jonas Keene had stopped as if he'd stepped on a burr. He touched Scot's arm, and he said softly, "Might be some live ones closer'n we think. Listen to that curlew."

Scot and Bearpaw Mike listened. A curlew was sounding from a point upriver, its plaintive, limpid two-toned cry hanging in the air for a moment.

"Curlew," Bearpaw Mike murmured, "only it ain't a curlew at all; it's a damn Blackfoot curlew. Reckon they seen us, Jonas."

"Them ducks." Jonas nodded.

Another curlew sounded from across the river, and then a third downriver.

"They move fast," Bearpaw Mike said. "This hoss is fer gettin' the hell out o' here."

"They don't like three guns and three mountain men handling them," Scot said. He pointed to a knoll back off the river about fifty yards. It was treeless, grassy, with a

172

bald spot on top. "We'll get out in open country so we can see them when they come."

"Damn ducks," Jonas Keene said again, and they left the river, running at a sharp trot for the knoll.

The curlew upriver called urgently, excitement in its voice.

"Smellin' blood," Mike Malone said. "Only they ain't gettin' this boy's blood!"

They went up to the top of the knoll, making the last dozen yards at a fast run, and then dropped flat on the ground. Scot said, "I'll shoot first if they come. You boys hold your fire."

He had his rifle ready, but he took the pistol out of his belt and placed it, loaded, at his side. Jonas Keene and Mike Malone took their pistols out, also, along with their Green River knives, sticking the knives in the ground.

"We'll take a heap o' killin'," Jonas said with satisfaction. "Even Blackfeet don't like to run into trappers' guns if they kin help it. They like better odds."

The curlews had stopped crying, and nothing moved down along the water's edge. The timber had run out here, and any Indians coming from the direction of the river had to cross open ground. The three men lying flat on the knoll made poor targets, only the tops of their heads showing.

"They was figurin' on layin' an ambush fer us," Mike Malone observed, "an' we walked out of it. Now they'll have to talk over what they'll do."

"Never met an Injun didn't like to talk more'n fight," Jonas chuckled. "They'll come, though. Three scalps is three scalps, an' yours they been after a long time, Mike."

"Like it, myself," Mike grunted.

Scot pointed toward an island downriver, and they saw a file of riders crossing the river just below the island, going up on a sand bar in mid-river where the water was shallow, and then crossing to their side.

"Some of 'em," Jonas murmured. "Here's more."

A group of a dozen came out of the timber to the north of them, their ponies prancing as if they had been resting for some time and were anxious to run. The late-afternoon sun glinted on steel-tipped lances and bits of mirror entwined in the ponies' tails and manes.

"Ain't more than four guns in that bunch," Bearpaw Mike said contemptuously. "Nor'west fusils. We kin stand 'em off with rifles."

The dozen from the timber approached the knoll carefully, keeping out of rifle shot, evidently waiting for the other band to come up from the south. Scot had counted twenty or twenty-five in the group that had crossed the river.

"Likely a huntin' party," Jonas observed, "an' now they found somethin' worth huntin'. They'll have a try at us, I'm thinkin'."

The second band from the river swung out of the timber to the south and came on at a fast gallop straight toward the knoll. They rode very fast, and then they stopped out of rifle range.

"Allus like to put on a show," Mike Malone chuckled. "They'll fight, though, an' we'll leave a few o' 'em fer wolf bait."

174

...he Blackfeet drew back in the shade
...f them dismounting. Now and then
...orward on foot, brandishing his bow
...ng boasts and insults, but remaining
...A few others tried to crawl forward
...grass to get up close enough for a shot,
...e picked one of them off neatly, and
...p.

...fer the wolves," Jonas said with satis-
...ary a one of us touched."

...e squinted up at the sun. "Another three
...unset," he said. "Might be needin' a little
.... You boys let me know if they're comin'

...'t comin'," Jonas told him.

...Mike grunted, pushed his rifle to one side,
...s face down on his arms. In a matter of sec-
...vas snoring lustily.

...Keene sat up to stretch himself, and then he
...and walked around on the knoll in full sight of
...ans below. When he sat down again he nodded
...sleeping man and he said to Scot, "Reckon
...aw kin git through if that's the way your stick
...s. He kin crawl under the belly of a snake an' the
...e wouldn't know it."

...ot nodded.

...They'll be comin' up closer soon's it gits dark," Jonas
...d him. "Maybe in the mornin' they'll be close enough
...shoot us full o' arrows."

..."They won't find us here in the morning," Scot said.

..."Tell me about it."

Two young Indians suddenly darted out from the band coming upriver and raced their ponies up the grassy slope toward the knoll.

"Showin' off," Jonas said.

Scot leveled his rifle, held it steady on the Blackfoot to the fore, and then as the Indian swerved his pony at a distance of less than seventy-five yards, he squeezed gently on the trigger.

The rifle bucked against his shoulder and the Indian fell forward, grasping at the pony's mane to hold himself from falling to the ground. A few more bounds and he slipped off into the grass. He got up and tried to run, but he was wobbling badly, and he hadn't taken more than five steps before he went down again, making no move this time.

"Good shootin'," Bearpaw Mike said.

The Blackfeet were yelling angrily, cavorting on their horses, but making no attempts to come closer. The second man who had made that foolish charge had whirled his pony and gone back to the others.

Scot reloaded the rifle while Jonas Keene and Bearpaw Mike kept theirs in readiness. The Blackfeet had withdrawn a little, and quite a number of them had dismounted.

"Makin' medicine," Mike Malone said." Gittin' out their special little gods an' paintin' their faces. They got to work up their courage some way."

"Here they come," Scot said.

Both bands were moving up now, sweeping out wide, forming two semicircles as they approached the knoll from the north and the south. They chanted as they moved their ponies at a slow trot, gradually picking up speed as they drew closer. When they came within rifle shot they were moving at top speed.

Jonas Keene said, "Hold your fire, boys."

He leveled his rifle, cocked his head as he lay flat on his stomach, and then the gun spat viciously. An Indian on a pure-black horse threw up his arms and fell to the grass. The others slowed down, yelling in rage.

The party coming up from the south stopped also when Mike Malone's gun spoke, and another Blackfoot slumped forward on his pony's neck to slide to the ground and be dragged along by the halter rope attached to his ankle.

Both trappers reloaded hastily as Scot kept his rifle in readiness, but the Blackfeet had drawn off again after picking up the two men who had been shot from their ponies.

"They ain't likin' this," Jonas said. "Reckon they know now they ain't up against pork-eaters."

"They're not finished," Scot told him. "They'll stick around a long while."

"Seen 'em hang on fer a week fer one scalp," Bearpaw Mike said. "Only we ain't sittin' here that long."

"You figure a way to git out," Jonas chided, "when they draw a circle around us tonight."

"Ain't an Injun east o' the mountains I can't crawl past," Bearpaw Mike boasted.

"One of us might get past them," Scot said thoughtfully. "Three never would."

"Odds agin' it," Jonas agreed.

The three men were silent as they lay on the knoll, the

hot sun beating down o
river from where
flowed slu
away, but t

"This hoss
Mike murmur

"Comanches
Jonas Keene said

"You was young
"What happened
"I died," Jonas Ke
Bearpaw Mike whoo
feet on their ponies star

"Come nightfall," Jona
that river, Scot, an' maybe
on."

"The three of us would
sounding an alarm."

"Ain't much choice," Jonas o
hell out o' here tonight, then
tomorrow."

"He's right," Mike Malone said.
bust through 'em, Scot, an' pick
hosses? They owe me some anyhow.'

"They'd follow us downriver," Scot s
able to get away, and they'd bring a larg
our camp. We're not prepared for a larg
yet."

Mike Malone nodded soberly. "Makes
admitted. "I figure I kin still git through, thoug

"Might have your chance." Scot told him.

They lay there as t
of the trees, most o
one of them came
or his gun, shouti
out of rifle shot.
through the low
but Mike Malo
they gave that u
"Four of 'em
factions "and
Mike Malo
hours afore s
sleep tonigh
again."
"They ai
Bearpaw
and put h
onds he
Jonas
stood u
the Indi
to the
Bearp
point
snak
S

tol
to

"We'll let Bearpaw go through after some of the Blackfeet horses down in the timber," Scot explained. "When he starts to drive them away, making a lot of noise, it should pull most of the Blackfeet away from this knoll. They'll think the three of us have crawled out."

"Makes sense," Jonas agreed.

"You and I will move down to the river and select a dead driftwood tree along the beach. We'll get it into the water and let the current take us downstream."

"What about Mike?"

"He'll drive off a few of the ponies, but he won't go with them. He can make his way down to the river a few hundred yards below and join us while the Blackfeet are chasing their ponies."

Jonas Keene grinned. "Should work," he said. "Now you kin use a few hours' sleep, Scot. You ain't had too much o' late. Wake you when it gits dark."

"Obliged," Scot murmured. He rolled over on his back, pulled his hat across his face to shade it from the sun, and lay still. He could hear the hum of insects in the grass now that the shooting had stopped and the Blackfeet had drawn off. Geese honked as they passed by along the river high overhead. The sun was warm on his body. He lay still, completely relaxed, forgetting for the moment the Blackfeet waiting below to kill him and take his scalp. He thought of Nanette and himself, and then of Lucien Weatherby and Carole Du Bois, and he was amazed at the way their affairs had worked out. He had thought he was in love with Carole, but Nanette had kept getting into the way, and he knew now that it had been Nanette ever since that first night when she had been found aboard the Osage.

Sleep came to him slowly. He could hear Bearpaw Mike Malone snoring at his side, and the curlews calling on the river—real curlews this time. Far off in the distance a wolf pack barked as it went after a stray buffalo or a single antelope it had singled out from the herd.

He felt his body pressing deeper and deeper into the ground. His eyelids became very heavy. Sound and sight and senses became torpid, and then he heard Jonas Keene's soft voice:

"Rise an' shine, gents."

## Chapter Fifteen

Scot sat up immediately, slipping the hat onto his head. It was fully dark, and he could see the stars crowding into the sky overhead. It had become considerably colder with the sun gone down, and he was stiff after his few hours' sleep.

Mike Malone was already awake, squatting, rising, and squatting again, as he brought the circulation back into his legs. Jonas Keene had his rifle in readiness, and he was peering into the darkness around them.

"They comin' in?" Bearpaw Mike asked. "

"Reckon they made their circle around this knoll already," Jonas said. "This hoss kin see like an owl in the dark, an' they ain't comin' too close without gettin' some lead into 'em."

Mike said to Scot, "I'll move out when you're ready."

"Think you can make it?" Scot asked him.

180

He heard the big man's low laugh. "I'll take some Blackfoot hair as I go along," Mike boasted.

"Hell with the hair," Jonas said. "Git them horses runnin' down below."

"When?" Bearpaw Mike asked.

"Another hour," Scot told him. "Give them time to get set."

"We'll look fer you a half mile down the river," Jonas said. "You hear a nighthawk, come swimmin'."

"One o' you boys better carry my rifle," Mike said. "Won't be needin' it. Have a pistol an' a knife. Knife will be best."

"Here's one of 'em comin' in too close," Jonas Keene whispered, and he lifted his rifle with one easy motion and fired it.

There was a yell of pain fifty or sixty yards down the slope, and then they could hear moccasins breaking through the tall grass below.

"Wouldn't be able to yell if I'd got him right," Jonas growled. "Eyesight's gittin' bad."

Scot hadn't even seen the Indian below. Fierce shouts came from points all around them after the shot.

"They ain't likin' that," Mike Malone chuckled, "but it'll keep 'em down a ways."

Jonas reloaded his rifle, and then he said, "Bunch back at the camp is likely worryin' about us now, Scot. Be hell on them if the Blackfeet rubbed us out."

"Take more'n a Blackfoot to rub out Bearpaw Mike," the big man stated.

They lay still for some time on the knoll, listening, saying nothing. After a while Mike Malone said, "If I

181

don't make it, that rifle goes to Weatherby. Good man, that Weatherby, fer all his drawin' pitchers an' his soft talk. He'd make a good mountain man if he put his mind to it."

"Time to go," Jonas Keene said.

Scot felt Mike Malone's rifle pressed into his hands, and Bearpaw Mike said, "You boys keep talkin' so they'll think the three of us are still here."

"Half mile downriver," Jonas murmured. "Cry o' the nighthawk."

"Luck," Mike Malone murmured.

"Luck," Scot said, and then Bearpaw Mike was gone.

Jonas Keene started to talk in unnecessarily loud tones that carried down the grade, and then Scot joined him, but both men were listening carefully, waiting for an outcry that would tell them that Mike Malone had been intercepted.

"Might take him an hour to git through," Jonas whispered. "Mike takes his time."

"We have time." Scot smiled wryly. He had a mental picture of the big redhead sliding inch by inch down this slope, scarcely breathing, having to pass within yards or feet of watching Indian sentinels who wanted his scalp more than the scalp of any other mountain man in the West.

"We'll hear it if they ketch him," Jonas said, "an' if they do I'm goin' down there."

"I'll be with you," Scot told him.

Nearly an hour passed and they heard nothing. They continued to talk, and once Jonas broke out into song to let the Blackfeet know that they were still on the knoll.

182

"When we hear the noise down there," Scot murmured, "we'll give this bunch around the knoll a few minutes to get away. Then we'll head for the river."

They remained quiet now, keeping down low on the knoll so that they couldn't be seen, and they waited. They had to give the Blackfeet the impression now that they were making their way down the grade and through the ring of watchers, so that when the shooting broke out below, the Indians would think all three had escaped.

Another half hour passed, and Jonas Keene said softly, "Mike's takin' his damn time about it."

Then they heard a pistol shot and several wild whoops from the timber south of them along the river. They had seen the Blackfeet hobble their ponies along the fringe of wood there.

More pistol shots followed, and they could hear horses running and leaping away across the open plains to the east of them. A bull-like voice kept after the ponies, and then the Blackfeet started to yell. Several rifles were fired, and they could see the flash of the guns in the darkness below.

Blackfeet below them were springing to their feet and running in the direction of the shooting.

"Move off here," Jonas Keene whispered, and they crawled from the knoll, moving fifteen or twenty yards before stopping and lying still in the grass.

They could hear Indians running past them in the darkness, and one came within ten feet of Scot as he lay on his stomach, his knife in his hand. Mounted Indians raced over the top of the knoll where they had been lying, heading down the other side after the ponies that

183

Mike Malone had attempted to run off.

There was more shooting from the south, and occasional wild whoops, followed by Mike Malone's bull-like roar.

"He's givin' 'em hell." Jonas chuckled. "Ready to go, Scot?"

Scot picked up the two rifles and they started down the slope toward the river, running fast and crouching a little as they ran. They had taken less than a dozen steps when a dark figure swung toward them from the north. Scot caught the Indian smell and he dropped the rifles immediately. He heard Jonas Keene grunt under his breath and then swerve in the direction of the Indian without breaking his pace. The downward slope gave him momentum, and he hit the Indian moving at top speed.

Scot heard the Blackfoot's stifled yelp of astonishment as he went down in the grass with the lean hunter on top of him. They rolled over and over as they went down the hill, and Scot snatched up his rifles again to follow them.

The Indian let out another short, muffled yell that did not carry more than a dozen yards, and it ended in a sickening gurgling sound. Jonas had found his throat with the knife in his hand.

Jonas was rising to his feet when Scot reached him, and they ran on down to the beach and quickly located a drift-wood log half up on the sand and half in the water. They worked rapidly, dragging the log out into the deeper water, making as little noise as possible. When they had it floating in waist-deep water, both of them clambered on, holding to the dead limbs of the tree, which lifted up toward the night sky like skeleton fingers.

Flattening themselves against the log and holding on to some of the dead branches, they let the current take them slowly downstream. Off to the east they could hear the Blackfeet whooping as they tried to round up their stampeded ponies.

Jonas said softly, "You figure Bearpaw was able to swing around 'em, Scot?"

"We'll know in a few minutes," Scot said.

They drifted about thirty or forty yards from the east bank of the river, moving very slowly, watching the tall trees go by. When they were about a half mile from the place where they had embarked, Jonas Keene lifted his head slightly and gave the sharp, piercing cry of a nighthawk.

An answering cry came from the bank a short distance downstream, and Jonas chuckled in his throat. A few minutes later Mike Malone hoisted himself up on the dead tree and lay there, breathing hard.

"All right, hoss?" Jonas asked him.

"I'm here," Mike grunted. "Cut a couple o' hobbles on them ponies an' run 'em off to the east. I was ridin' one of 'em, an' then I slipped off an' cut back to the river. Injuns kept goin'."

"We're obliged to you, Mike," Scot told him.

"We stayin' on this tree all the way down to the camp?" Jonas asked.

"Safer than going ashore," Scot said. "Blackfeet won't be looking for us out on the river."

They drifted silently downstream, making themselves as comfortable as possible on the drifting tree.

"Reckon we found out what we came to find out,

anyway," Mike Malone said.

"Plenty Blackfeet in this part o' the country," Jonas agreed. "All Bloods, too. We have to git on the right side o' the Piegans, Scot."

"We'll find them," Scot said. "When we get the post set up and the trade goods on display, they'll come in."

"Ever figure how to tell a Blood an' a Piegan apart?" Bearpaw Mike asked.

"How?" Jonas wanted to know.

"Blood takes your hair soon's he sees it." Mike Malone grinned. "Piegan thinks about it a little, then takes it."

They drifted down the river, once or twice snagging against small islands, where they had to get off the drift log and push it clear again. They saw no more of the Blackfeet who had besieged them, and eventually they swung around a small bend and came down toward the beach where the Osage had tied up earlier in the day.

They could see the keelboat, a dull shadow against the bank, and then the glow of the campfire coals beyond it on the shore. Scot stood up on the drifting tree, gripping some of the dead branches. He called in a low voice, "Osage. Osage."

Someone kicked up the fire a little, providing more light, and several dark figures moved down toward the shore as they worked the drifting tree in closer to the sand.

"Reckon we kin let her go here," Jonas said, "an' swim in."

Bearpaw Mike lowered himself into the water and found that it came up to his shoulders.

"We kin walk in," he said, "without gettin' the rifles wet."

Scot was looking at the Osage as they came in closer to the boat. He could see figures moving on the deck, probably Nanette and Carole. He called again, "Osage?"

"Come in," someone called back, the voice muffled.

The three of them started to wade in, holding the rifles over their heads, watching for potholes in the river. Scot noticed that more of the crew were coming down to the water's edge. He could see their figures outlined against the rising flames of the fire, but he missed the giant shape of Baptiste Privot and the lean, small figure of Lucien Weatherby.

Jonas Keene had become aware of the fact that Weatherby wasn't on the shore, either, and he said, "Reckon Lucien got worried about us an' took some o' the boys to scout up the river. Don't see Baptiste, either."

Scot frowned a little. It had not been a particularly wise move for both lieutenants to leave the camp and look for them. A surprise Indian attack would have panicked the Creoles without a leader.

He thought he recognized one figure on the beach—a big, broad-shouldered man, standing with legs apart. That would be Romaine, the cook, the biggest man in the outfit next to Baptiste Privot.

"Git that meat pot boilin'," Bearpaw Mike called. "We ain't et since noon, an' this hoss kin eat a Blackfoot with the hair on him."

There was no response from the men on the beach. The big man who should have been Romaine didn't hurry back to the campfire. He stood there, silhouetted against the flames, as they waded into water up to their knees and came on to the shore.

Scot stopped when he was a dozen paces from the silent crew on the shore. Something was very definitely wrong here. The Creoles should have been excited and happy over the return of the bourgeois. They were like small children, always giving way to their emotions, but now they said nothing. They waited, a dozen of them. He did not hear Nanette's glad voice, either, even though there were figures up in the bow of the Osage.

Jonas Keene had stopped, also, but Bearpaw Mike continued to wade in toward the shore, stopping only when he noticed that Scot and Jonas were no longer with him. He turned, then, and he said, "Cold river, boys. Come on out."

"Come easy," the big man on the shore said, "and come with your hands over your head. Drop those rifles in the water."

The voice was not the voice of Romaine. It was another voice—a familiar voice that Scot MacGregor had hoped he would never hear again up in this north country. It was the voice of Cass Brandon.

## Chapter Sixteen

Jonas Keene spoke first after Brandon had given his order. Jonas said softly, "Reckon this fish came in to the wrong shore, Scot."

"Drop the rifles," Brandon snapped. "You're covered all along the shore here, and we have that swivel gun trained on you from the boat."

Mike Malone cursed under his breath and looked back at Scot. Scot was staring at Brandon, bitterness running through him. He had tried to help this man to get back to civilization after his boat had been burned by the Blackfeet. He had helped him even though he knew that Brandon had tried to ruin him earlier on the trip. This was the way Brandon was paying him back.

"Walk in," Brandon ordered, a note of triumph in his voice. "Drop the rifles into the water."

"Git wet," Bearpaw Mike snarled. "This is the best damned gun on the river, Brandon."

Orange flame spurted from the pistol in Brandon's hand, the ball striking the water close by Mike Malone, raising a small geyser. The mountain man's rifle hit the water with a splash. Jonas dropped his, and then Scot let his own gun fall into the water at his feet. He walked forward then, knowing that it was useless to resist.

"Reckon you got the drop on us," Jonas Keene said tightly. "Better keep it that way, Brandon."

Scot came out on the shore, river water dripping from him. He looked at Brandon, who had turned slightly so that the firelight played on his broad face now. His green eyes were shining like the eyes of an animal, and he was grinning.

"You figure I'd really go downriver, Scot?" he asked.

Scot just looked at him. He looked beyond Brandon, and then he saw his own men sitting on the ground back in the shadows beyond the firelight, a number of Brandon's crew guarding them with rifles. He said, "Where are Weatherby and Baptiste Privot?"

He had this one hope yet, that Weatherby had really

gone out with part of the crew to search for him, and Brandon had taken over the boat while the artist was gone.

"Both of them trussed up aboard the Osage," Brandon told him.

Scot said nothing. A feeling akin to physical sickness went over him. They had reached their destination, the farthest north any keelboat had ever gone before. They were in Blackfoot country and still alive, their valuable cargo intact, and now all was gone.

He knew now that he had made his mistake in taking both trappers along with him on this brief scouting expedition up the river. If he had left either one at the camp, Brandon probably could not have come upon them unawares.

Scot walked past Brandon toward the campfire. He said over his shoulder, "This is piracy, Brandon. You'll never get away with it. They'll hang you back in St. Louis."

He stood there by the fire, noticing that the first faint streaks of light were coming into the sky beyond the fringe of timber. Another day was coming.

"I'll worry about St. Louis," Brandon laughed, "when I get there." He said to the crew, "Tie them up, and make sure you take their knives and pistols."

"I kin cut through rope with my teeth," Bearpaw Mike growled.

"Not if they're knocked out." Brandon smiled. "Watch your tongue, trapper."

"Cut yours out," Mike Malone murmured. "Should o' done it years ago, Brandon. I'll eat it, too."

hot coffee from the pot. Jonas Keene started to
ⁿftly, persistently.

't concern yourself with them," Brandon advised

poured another cup and came over to hand it to
Then she looked down at Scot directly for the first
and she said sneeringly, "*Mon Dieu!* He told me
ⁿe loved me! He kissed me!"

e spat, and Cass Brandon grinned. He said to Scot,
ⁿer found out who fired your boat back at Leaven-
ⁿth did you, or who cut through your cordelle line at
*embarras?*"

ⁿcot didn't say anything. He was still staring at
ⁿanette, the full realization of what she had done begin-
ⁿng to come to him. All the while she had been acting
ⁿhen he caught her running upriver to Brandon. She had
ⁿeen returning to him because she loved him, and she
ⁿad given Scot her story because she knew he suspected
ⁿer. She had been acting beautifully, telling him the truth
because the truth would disarm him. And all the while it
had been Brandon. He remembered now that she had
looked back downriver when they left Brandon on the
beach, and she had gone along with him, pretending that
she loved him, seeking another chance to ruin him so
that she could go to Brandon.

Scot said slowly, "I know who fired my boat,
Brandon." He was looking at Nanette, watching her sip
the hot coffee. She stood a few feet from him, legs
spread a little, one hand on her hip. She was wearing the
boy's pants and a white silk blouse from the trade goods,
and she made a fetching figure, her black hair, short and

Brandon stepped up to him and slashed viciously with
the barrel of his pistol. The move was unexpected. Mike
Malone attempted to leap back, but the pistol caught
him on the side of the head, dropping him to the sand. A
trickle of dark blood slid down his cheek.

"Tie them up," Brandon snapped.

His tough Creole crewmen came up with pieces of
rope. One of them yanked Scot's arms behind his back
and fastened his wrists tightly with the rope. Another
man knelt down over Mike Malone, rolled him on his
stomach, and then bound him tightly.

The three of them were forced to sit down near the
fire. Jonas Keene looked across at Scot and shook his
head in disgust. Mike Malone came back to conscious-
ness and stared around stupidly for a moment, the blood
still dripping from his chin.

Brandon stood by the fire, packing his pipe. He said to
Scot, "You didn't figure I'd go downriver without fur,
Scot?"

Scot just looked at him. "What's your play?" he asked.
"You know damn well you can't take a stolen keelboat
back to St. Louis. There would be questions even at
Leavenworth.

Brandon shrugged. "We don't have to go back to St.
Louis with the Osage," he pointed out. "When we've
collected our furs we can pick up Indian ponies down-
river and come in as a fur brigade. We'll burn your
Osage before we reach Leavenworth and tell them the
Sioux or Blackfeet got our boat.

"What about us?" Scot asked.

Brandon puffed on the pipe after putting a coal into the

bowl. "Could be they rubbed you out, too," he murmured. "Likely up here, isn't it?"

Scot didn't answer. He stared at this big, blond man with the smooth-shaven face, a handsome man with a devil in his heart. It did not seem possible that Brandon would deliberately murder all of his captives—over thirty men and two women.

"Your company," Scot said, "wouldn't stand for a deal like this, Brandon. They'll hear of it."

"To hell with my company." Brandon laughed. "The Blackfeet burned the company boat and all the trade goods. This is my own deal. I'll find a buyer outside of St. Louis, and then go downriver with the profits. The boys with me stand to make ten times what they'd receive as wages for the company. They're with me."

"Blackfeet'll rub you out," Jonas Keene told him. "You ain't downriver yet, hoss, an' you ain't took a single pelt."

"We'll have plenty beaver when we go home." Brandon grinned. "Blackfeet are our friends, and we're the only boat upriver this summer."

"The Blackfeet don't have friends," Jonas said.

"We'll see," Brandon said, and it was as if he were in possession of information that infinitely pleased him.

Scot watched him turn and head toward the Osage. A few minutes later Baptiste Privot and Lucien Weatherby were led down the plank, their hands tied behind them. They were pushed up toward the fire, and Weatherby looked down at Scot, regret in his face. He said before he sat down awkwardly, "They hit us earlier in the evening, Scot. Some of the guards either fell asleep or

were surprised by Brandon's [...] walked into the camp with their g[...] a chance to fight."

"Where are Nanette and Carole?[...]

"Locked in the cabin."

"This Brandon I will kill," Baptiste [...]

"You run into trouble, too?" Weathe[...]

"Blackfoot trouble," Scot told him. [...] sketch of their run-in with the Blackfeet, [...] shook his head sympathetically.

"He has us, Scot," he murmured. "I'm [...] what he plans to do with us."

"He's taking the Osage and the cargo," Sc[...]

"He can't take us," Weatherby observed. "[...] And he can't leave us here."

Scot looked at him. "Why not?" he said.

He saw Weatherby's lean face go pale, and th[...] tiste Privot, who had been listening, said slowly, [...] *Dieu!*"

Brandon was still aboard the Osage after having [...] Baptiste and Weatherby ashore. He came back now [...] Nanette La Rue, and Scot noticed that Carole was [...] with them.

Nanette was not tied. She walked ashore and came u[...] to the fire, and then she looked down at Scot with very [...] little interest in her eyes. Scot stared back at her, uncomprehending for a moment.

Nanette said to Brandon, "What shall we do with these peegs, *mon cher?*"

Scot's lower jaw sagged a little as he stared at the girl. She walked insolently around the fire and poured herself

a cup of[...]
curse s[...]
"Do[...]
her.
She [...]
him. [...]
time, [...]
that [...]
Sh[...]
"Ne[...]
wo[...]
the[...]
N[...]
ni[...]
w[...]
h[...]

curly, blowing slightly in the breeze coming up with the dawn.

Brandon put his arm around Nanette's waist as he finished his coffee. He said, "You were easy to fool, MacGregor. Did you really think my Nanette was in love with you?"

"Nanette loves no one but herself," Scot said dully.

"Peeg!" Nanette snarled, and she stepped forward to throw the dregs of the cup full in his face as he sat on the ground, hands tied behind him.

"Worse'n a Blackfoot squaw," Jonas Keene whispered. "Should o' let the Blackfeet have her the other night, Scot."

Scot didn't say anything. He sat there with the hot coffee dripping from his chin, staring straight ahead of him, wondering how he could have been such a fool. He had given up a girl like Carole Du Bois for this common baggage from New Orleans and St. Louis.

Lucien Weatherby was saying to Brandon, "Where is Miss Du Bois?"

"Cabin," Brandon told him.

"You harm that girl," Weatherby said, "and I'll kill you, Brandon."

Brandon looked down at him speculatingly, and then he said, "You gentlemen don't seem to realize your predicament. You're not in a position to make threats, Weatherby."

"I still mean it," the artist stated, his voice tense with emotion.

"Figured on taking Miss Du Bois with me." Brandon grinned. "A little extra female company on board the

195

Osage wouldn't hurt."

"*Non*," Nanette said emphatically. "I do not like her."

Cass Brandon pointed a finger at his chest. "I make the decisions who I like and don't like," he said.

Nanette pouted and walked off down along the shore. More light was coming into the sky. It changed from dull white to yellow and then to red in the east, and gradually the sun touched the tops of the trees on the far shore of the river.

Brandon's crew cooked their breakfast, and they released one man at a time, enabling him to eat before tying him up again. The Osage crew, stupefied by what had happened, and apprehensive of the future, sat on the shore staring at each other, rifles trained on them all the time.

Jonas Keene said to Scot as they sat side by side near the fire, "Reckon they had no trouble catchin' up with us, Scot, with all these damned bends in the river. A man could walk faster than a keelboat could go."

"Should have been watching for trouble," Scot said. "Didn't think he'd go this far, though."

Both men were silent for a few moments. Scot's eyes moved over toward Nanette, who was chatting with the boss-man of Brandon's crew, a lean, lantern-jawed Creole with lank black hair and a mustache. She was flirting with him outrageously.

Scot wondered how he could have been such a fool. He had to admit that she was devilishly clever, a consummate actress. He remembered how she had played the part of a fourteen-year-old boy back in St. Louis, and then her innocence and pretense the early part of the voyage upriver, her coquetry. Then she had become serious, pretending that she loved him, and pretending that she was running away from Brandon while she was really running back to him. Now he was seeing her in her true lights, a camp follower for a handsome, ruthless man.

After eating Brandon walked upriver a short distance with his hunter, a lean, rat-faced man who had lost one ear in a fight.

Jonas said to Scot, "He can't go more'n a mile or two upriver now, Scot, an' he'll have to use the cordelle line all the way."

Bearpaw Mike Malone, who was beginning to recover from the brutal blow on the head, said, "What's he figurin' on doin' with us, Jonas?"

"Nothin'," Jonas told him.

"Nothin'?"

"That's the way his stick points," Jonas growled. "We're just sittin' here as he moves upriver with the Osage an' his crew."

"Jest leavin' us be?" Mike muttered. "Don't sound like him."

"Without guns," Jonas added. "Without even a damn knife, an' the country swarmin' with Blackfeet. How long you figure we'll last, Mike?"

Lucien Weatherby had been listening, and he said slowly, "It's inhuman. Only a devil would do a thing like that."

"He's a devil," Jonas agreed, "an' in twenty-four hours, I'm thinkin', we'll be wolf bait."

Scot watched Baptiste Privot straining surreptitiously

at the ropes binding his wrists behind his back. Four crewmen were watching them with rifles as they sat on the ground, and Baptiste had to be careful, working only when they weren't looking in his direction.

Brandon came back to the fire, a satisfied expression on his face. He said to Scot, "We're moving upriver, MacGregor. Hope you're comfortable here."

Scot just looked at him, but didn't say anything. Jonas Keene said, "You're a dirty dog, Brandon."

Cass Brandon stepped over and kicked him full in the face, sending him rolling in the sand, his hands still tied behind his back. The left side of Jonas' face started to swell rapidly as he sat up again, his mild brown eyes mere slits now.

"You should have visitors a short while after we leave," Brandon said. "Treat them nicely."

He turned away then, and had a talk with his boss-man. They were plainly discussing the river, and the method they would use to propel the Osage away from this doomed beach.

Scot noticed that his own crewmen still weren't trussed up in any way. Brandon contemptuously gave them their freedom, although he kept men with rifles watching them all the time. They were sheep without a leader, and Brandon was preparing them for the slaughter now. They sat on the ground beyond the camp-fire, looking at their own leaders securely tied and help-less, and then at Brandon and his crew with the rifles and pistols, and with the swivel gun in the bow of the Osage trained on them.

Very definitely, Scot knew that they could expect no

help from his crew. Only Baptiste, still straining at the rope that tied his wrists, provided the smallest spark of hope. The veins in Baptiste's forehead stood out like cords as he strained every time the guards weren't watching him, but when he looked at Scot, Scot saw the despair in his dark eyes.

Even if the giant were able to break loose before the Osage left the shore, he was one man without a gun, without even a knife, and before he could free any of the others they would shoot him down.

Bearpaw Mike Malone said dully, "Reckon Brandon holds all the cards, boys, an' he's dealin' with a stacked deck."

Scot looked over at his crew, the sickness coming to him again. He could see them running with the Blackfeet pursuing them, striking them down. He had brought them a long way up this river to die, and dying with them was the hope that they would be able to establish the first permanent trading post up in this north country, the first steppingstone to the unopened Oregon Territory.

Lucien Weatherby was staring at the Osage, where Carole Du Bois was held prisoner, a guard with a rifle watching the cabin door. She was a brave girl, but helpless to assist them now. Weatherby was dying a slow death as Cass Brandon made ready to pole the keelboat away from the shore.

The crew began taking out the cordelle line, and Brandon was giving his final instructions. He walked over toward the spot where Scot's crew was sitting, watching him dumbly, and he spoke to them in French. Scot could hear what he was saying, warning them not

199

to make a move until the Osage was out of sight, or he would come back and blow them to pieces with the swivel gun.

Brandon sent twenty men upriver with the cordelle line, while the remaining ten went on board the Osage. Three of them went to the swivel gun, which was still trained on the shore.

Scot, Jonas Keene, Mike Malone, and Baptiste Privot sat around the dying cook fire, hands still bound behind their backs. Baptiste was straining again, his face distorted and flushed with the effort, but the cords still held.

Just before the planks were pulled away, Nanette came off the Osage. Brandon had walked a short distance upriver, watching the men with the cordelle line as they towed it along the shore. He came back now, and Nanette fell in step with him.

Scot could hear her talking, and there was some sharpness in her voice. He heard Carole's name mentioned, and it was evident that she was still arguing with Brandon, trying to persuade him to leave Carole behind.

"She ain't carin'," Jonas Keene growled, "if the Blackfeet git Carole, too. She has to be head woman up here."

"*Sacrebleu!*" Baptiste Privot whispered to the Creole crew behind him. "Peegs! Romaine, Gaston, Garand. The ropes!"

The Creoles looked at each other, and then at the swivel gun on the deck, and then at Brandon, who had paused by the plank just before crossing to the deck. They made no move.

Nanette was still remonstrating with Brandon as they

stood by the plank, and Brandon was shaking his head. When he looked up and spoke to one of the crew on the boat, Nanette stepped aside. She looked straight at Scot, seated on the ground less than fifteen feet away. She said nothing and she made no movement. There was no particular expression on her face, but Scot had the queer feeling that she was trying to convey a message to him without attracting Brandon's attention.

It was ridiculous, of course, for the moment Brandon turned around she was at him again, sidling up to him, pleading with him. She put her arms around him and looked up into his face, and Scot stared down intently at the sand.

Then he heard Jonas Keene's sharp intake of breath. He looked up just in time to see the knife in Nanette's hand sliding into the small of Cass Brandon's back.

For one brief moment the bright morning sunlight gleamed on the knife blade, and then it was gone. She was still holding Brandon with her left arm, but with the right she had slipped the knife from inside the waistband of the boy's pants she was wearing, and had calmly plunged it into his back.

Brandon had been looking down at her when the knife went home, and Scot saw the expression on his face change from conceited vanity to mock incredulity. His knees started to sag, and he opened his mouth as if he wanted to say something, but couldn't find the proper words: He wanted to lift his hands, also, but it was as if they were held down by heavy weights, and he couldn't bring them above his waist.

Nanette had stepped back, the knife still in her hand,

and she reached forward now, sliding the pistol from his belt as he staggered forward and started to fall. Turning, she ran at top speed to the fire with the gun in one hand and the knife in the other.

Reaching Scot first, she crouched beside him and slashed through the cords binding his wrists. As Scot's hands came around to the front of him, she pushed the gun into his hands and said in a strangled voice, "Hurry."

Scot knew the reason for the haste now. Cass Brandon had pitched forward on his face in the sand and lay still, but the men around the swivel gun, after staring stupidly at him, were swinging the four-pounder toward the group of men on the beach. The lean, rat-faced hunter was shouting harshly at the clumsy Creoles manipulating the gun, trying to get them to hurry.

Lifting the pistol, Scot shot him through the head from a sitting position. Nanette had left him and was moving from Jonas Keene to Bearpaw Mike Malone and then to Baptiste Privot, slashing their bonds, freeing them.

Big Mike Malone rose with a whoop and lunged toward the plank, Jonas Keene following him. Baptiste Privot went through the shallow water like a great terrier, and the three of them reached the deck of the Osage at about the same time.

The cannon boomed, but it had been aimed hastily and the shot went wild, clipping branches from the trees above where the Creoles still sat. Bearpaw Mike Malone grabbed one of the gunners, lifted him into the air, and crashed him down on the deck, senseless.

Baptiste Privot's huge arms encircled two other men, and he drew them in toward his chest in a terrible bearhug. The men screamed, and when he released them they dropped to the deck, gasping, as weak as kittens.

A half dozen others of Brandon's crew had been waiting with the long poles, ready to pole the Osage away from the shore when the last rope was untied.

Scot and Lucien Weatherby raced aboard then, followed by a few of the crew, who had taken courage now that the fight was joined. The men with the poles were unarmed, and they made little resistance when Mike Malone and Baptiste Privot came at them. Several jumped into the river. The others dropped their poles, pleading for mercy.

"Get the rifles out of the cabin," Scot ordered. He noticed that Jonas Keene was already at the swivel gun, reloading it, pointing it upriver, where twenty of Brandon's crew had been dragging the cordelle line. They had stopped and were staring back at the boat from a distance of about seventy-five yards. Most of these men carried arms for fear of Indian attack along the shore, and they started to shoot at the boat.

Baptiste Privot roared at their own Creoles to come aboard for guns, and the Osage crew responded now, yelling happily, seeing victory.

The little four-pounder roared and the shot crashed in among the trees close by Brandon's crew. Rifles started to crack all along the deck. Carole Du Bois was in the cabin doorway, handing out the guns, and it was only a matter of a few moments before the cordelle men broke and scattered among the trees for protection. With Brandon dead there was no force and no direction to them.

The Creoles were cheering lustily, realizing that they had recaptured the boat. Bearpaw Mike Malone was saying, "Where's that little gal? Where's that little gal?"

Scot saw her still on the shore. Nanette had cut Lucien Weatherby loose and then dropped the knife into the sand. She was sitting on a stone near the dying fire now, looking down at the ground.

Cass Brandon lay on his face a dozen yards from where she sat, arms and legs sprawled, the sand stained red underneath him. His hat had fallen from his head, and his golden hair was bright in the sunshine.

"Reckon she fooled him," Jonas Keene murmured. "All the while she was playin' her game, Scot. She had to make Brandon think she was with him."

Scot nodded. He went down the plank, passing Brandon, looking down at him for a moment, and then he went on to Nanette. Her face was pale and her eyes were dull when she looked up at him. He knew then what it had cost her to plunge a knife into a man's back while she was in his arms.

"I had to do it, *mon cher*," she whispered to Scot. "He wanted to kill all of you."

"I know," Scot nodded. He sat down beside her, putting his arm around her, holding her.

"You do not know," Nanette murmured, "that he sent a breed upriver to the Blackfeet to tell them there were men without guns at this place, and that they could take many scalps and they would not be hurt themselves. He was a devil, Scot."

Scot looked up at Jonas Keene, who had drawn near

and heard this bit of information. Jonas' mouth was tight, and he shook his head as if unable to believe that any man would go that far.

"Reckon that was the way he figured he'd get in solid with the Blackfeet," Jonas growled. "He told 'em we were bad men an' he was their friend. That would bring in the furs if he helped them take a heap o' scalps."

"It's all over now," Scot said, and he looked down at Nanette.

"I do not like to throw coffee in your face," Nanette whispered.

"You kin throw it in my face every mornin' from now on," Jonas Keene said, and he walked away, leaving them alone.

"I do not like to make love to him," Nanette said, looking in Brandon's direction and shuddering.

"Where did you get the knife?" Scot asked her.

"From the boss-man," Nanette explained. "I tell him I want knife to fight Blackfeet if they come."

Scot saw Lucien Weatherby up on the deck talking with Carole, and then they came ashore. Jonas Keene was putting things in order on the boat.

Baptiste Privot came ashore, and he looked down at Nanette for some time in silence, and then he smiled broadly and bent down to kiss her on the forehead.

"*Chérie,*" he said softly, "you are very brave. Brave as—as Baptiste himself."

It was a very great compliment, the most magnificent Baptiste Privot could conceive. Scot stood up. He said to Baptiste, "Get the men working on the barricade. Tomorrow we cut trees for the post walls."

*"Oui,"* Baptiste grinned. "With teeth Baptiste cut down mighty trees."

Bearpaw Mike Malone came up, and he said to Scot, "That bunch got away ain't lastin' long in this country. Blackfeet'll gobble 'em up afore nightfall, I'm thinkin'."

"How many prisoners we take?" Scot asked him.

"Seven," Mike told him, "an' they're beggin' like hell to stay with us. Got 'em locked up in the stern."

A crewman on board suddenly let out a piercing yell. He jabbered frantically and pointed across the river.

"Everybody git rifles!" Jonas Keene roared.

Scot joined Jonas down on the shoreline. Across the river a dozen or more Indians had ridden out from among the trees and were sitting astride their magnificent little mounts, looking across the river. They made no sounds as they stared at the Osage, and the men along the banks.

Bearpaw Mike Malone said softly, "Piegans, Scot. If they was Bloods they wouldn't even o' showed themselves. There's yore trade if you kin get it."

Scot had a rifle in his hand. He handed the rifle to Jonas Keene and stepped forward, unarmed. Then he raised his right arm in a gesture of friendliness, the age-old gesture of the plains and mountains.

The Blackfeet on the opposite shore looked at him for some time, their ponies pawing the sand, moving restlessly up and down along the beach. The sunlight reflected on their gun barrels, guns they had received from traders to the far north in Canada.

The Blackfeet started to file back in among the trees

after having had their look, and then one rider hesitated, staring at them across the expanse of water. He rode a brown and white spotted pony, bigger than the usual Indian horses. Just before he disappeared he lifted his right hand and put it down.

Jonas Keene said, "There's a beginnin', Scot. Now let's git to work."

It was a beginning, Scot MacGregor realized. They had reached their goal, and a trading post was going up here in the wilderness where never before a white man had ventured. This was the first step. It took one man to blaze a trail—one man with an ax and a rifle, and with deep courage in his heart. Others would follow where one had dared to go. It took an ax and a rifle, and courage, and a woman, too, a woman who would kill for her man.

Scot MacGregor went back to his woman.

**Center Point Publishing**
600 Brooks Road ● PO Box 1
Thorndike ME 04986-0001 USA

(207) 568-3717

US & Canada:
1 800 929-9108